Shifter's Dance

Laura Hawks

DEDICATION

This book is dedicated to you, the readers, for whom writing wouldn't be as enjoyable.
I would also like to dedicate this to my mother, whom I miss more than words can describe.
Finally, I would like to dedicate this to my husband, who literally saved my life.
May you all find pleasure in this world, whether it be from your friends, family, or fur-babies. We only pass this way once, make it worthwhile.

Laura Hawks
*Soaring on Wings
One Story at a Time*

Further Reading:
Words For Warriors II: A Word Search Book
Balconies of New Orleans

YA Paranormal:
       Gumshoe and the Mysterious Mushrooms

(These books are Adult Themed)
Demon Trilogy: Demon's Kiss
               Demon's Dream
               Demon's Web

Spirit Walker's Thrillers: Shifter's Hope
                      Shifter's Pride
                      Shifter's Journey
Ghost and the Grimoire

Fractured Fairytales:
     Snow White and the Seven Cannibals
Valley View Mysteries: Flaming Retribution
                    Stalking the Stalker

ACKNOWLEDGMENTS

I would like to thank all of my friends, family and fans who sent good wishes and kept me in their thoughts during my medical crisis of late. Without your thoughts and prayers, this book might not have been published.

I would like to thank all of you for your notes, emails and posts. They are greatly appreciated.

I hope that after reading this novel, you will take time to let me know your thoughts. My platforms are located in the back of this book under About the Author.

I would also appreciate it very much if you left a review on Amazon and/or Goodreads.

Thank you for your patronage and friendship.

PROLOGUE

1877

Lily-Anne gasped, her arms clawing at air as she struggled. Fighting to breathe. Fighting to be free. Fighting for her very life. Occasionally, she'd hit a solid mass, but it did nothing to relieve her torment. Her endeavors were becoming weaker, her attempts to break away waning. She was dying and the realization was a complete surprise.

She'd see no more sunrises or sunsets. She'd no longer feel arms holding her in a loving embrace. She'd no longer be able to taste the sweet nectar of honey slipping down her throat. As she exerted the last of her energy trying to cling to life, she suddenly realized the truth of the saying that one's life flashed before one's eyes just before death. Brief glimmers of important moments during her time in this world appeared in her mind's eye.

She saw her youthful self, running through fields of wildflowers chasing fireflies and giggling as they lit up a twilight sky. The scene shifted to standing in front of an altar, the man she loved slipping a ring on her finger. The setting changed once again to her standing over her husband's coffin as dirt was shoveled upon it. Sadness still clung to her, but she'd be joining him soon. Her world was getting darker as memories continued to play in her mind. The location metamorphosed into watching the home she loved with her deceased husband fade into the distance as she rode away to a new world, a new opportunity.

She'd been hopeful to start a new life and put the despair of her husband's youthful demise behind her. Although the stagecoach was rough and uncomfortable, the journey was going to bring new opportunities her way. She was still young. Only twenty-seven and she had a world of living to do. How could she know she'd been duped? How could she know her hopeful chance was a ruse designed to bring about her very ruin? Her excitement turned to despair when she learned of the trap she'd found herself in with no recourse to escape.

She'd taken her last gulps of constricted air as

she was being murdered. She could only hope death would bring her the peace she so desperately sought.

Pierre Hills felt it. He knew when the last vestiges of life drained from her body and, despite the fact he didn't want to admit that he was a monster, he couldn't help but be pleased with his handiwork. She'd thought herself so high and mighty, too good for the likes of him or any of the other guys in Deadwood who would pay good money to be with her. Women were only good for two things: making meals and sex, and he could cook for himself. Ever since she'd arrived in Deadwood, she fought against the men who paid for the privilege to be with her, even if that payment was only in gold dust. How many times had she been given a black eye or busted lip for her insubordination?

Al Swearingen didn't know what to do with her. Problem girls like her could start riots or worse. He'd given her over to the Melodeon and told them to do with her as they pleased. Their solution? To strip her naked and throw her into the basement until she learned some humility. She wasn't the only one in that stinking hole, but he knew that she, like the others, would eventually break, and when they came out of the hell they'd been thrown into they were more manageable for service.

Pierre was one of the managers for the Melodeon. He should've just taken her out and tested her to make sure she was browbeaten enough to be aptly subtle for the mining men, but there was something about her, something in her eyes that said there was no way in hell she'd ever stop fighting to let men just use her as they wished. To prove his point, Pierre took her dirty, naked ass out of the hole, dunked her into a vat of ice-cold water to get the slop and smell off, before he dragged her through the busy, hungry-eyed males in the saloon into the upstairs room and flung her onto the bed. He'd have his way with her and see how well she responded.

He'd only planned on doing her, beating her up a bit because he knew she'd fight him, but the thrill of her weakening struggles while he was buried deep inside couldn't stop him from going all the way and squeezing the life out of her as he came, harder than he ever remembered coming before. She flopped around like a ragdoll as he continued to pump into her, his hands still wrapped around her throat.

When he finally stopped, Pierre looked down at Lily-Anne and licked his lips. She'd been pretty, once. Before the hole and starvation, as well as the bruises, scrapes and other abuse she'd endured since she arrived to Deadwood and the Badlands. It was only as he stared at her lifeless lump of flesh did he realize what he'd done.

Deadwood didn't have many laws, especially in the Badlands, thanks to Al Swearingen, who made sure the law stayed out of this part of town, but killing girls was one of the few rules even Al wouldn't stand for being broken. The girls were money even if they were bruised and beaten, but dead? They wouldn't bring in anything. It was a waste, and if anyone found out, he'd be tried for murder. He couldn't and wouldn't risk it. He had to do something. He *would* do something. He just had to think.

Chapter One

Present Day

The crowd was restless. Some had even departed early due to the abnormally chilly weather after the rain. It was unusual to be this cold in the middle of June for Deadwood, South Dakota, but not unheard of.

Chase White Bear had watched the previous professional bull riders go and he only needed to make a score of thirty-five in order to maintain a solid second place. If he used his preternatural strength and stamina for the event, he could be world champion, but that was too much attention for him or his tribal band of Lakota Sioux. He was already in the public eye too much for their tastes and it had taken a lot just to convince the elders to let him do this for a couple of years before going into deep seclusion from the outside world.

Use of his abilities in public, even if the humans wouldn't even be aware of it, was strictly prohibited. Besides, he wanted to do this on his own with no divine assistance. He had the skill. He had the ability. He didn't need his special gifts to aide him in winning. He held back because he couldn't afford to be too famous. He won enough purses to give him the money he needed to set aside for himself as well as his people. However, popularity would draw attention he couldn't afford to have.

Chase was nine hundred and thirty-four years old, though he only looked like he was thirty-five. Being famous, humans would eventually realize he wasn't growing older like they were. However, the thrill of getting on the back of a rank bull and holding on for dear life with one hand free for eight seconds excited him. And he was good at it. But then, Chase's spirit guide was a bison, as fierce and strong as any bull.

Granted, his needed score of thirty-five was not dependent on the bull scoring his share of the one-hundred points allotted for the event. The PBR Touring Pro Division arrived at the Days of '76 Rodeo Event Complex earlier. There were only forty slots opened for application to ride and try out for the final attempt tomorrow, where only ten spots were available in the short go-round. But Chase didn't care. He loved the scent of the bulls in their pens, some already itching for the opportunity to be in the chute. One-hundred points probably didn't seem like much to the outsiders, but to the gladiators of the arena, those eight seconds were almost a lifetime on the back of a bucking bull. The excitement and anticipation was evident from everyone waiting for their turn to head into the chute and climb onto the most rank bull they were assigned.

Chase rubbed his nose with the back of his hand. The strong smell of pain ointments made his nose itch and his eyes run slightly. It was one of the few things he didn't care for in the changing area. Humans needed all kinds of medical aides to slather on themselves to keep their aches and pains minimal. Native Americans learned eons ago more natural ways and certainly less odorous ones.

Again, Chase's eyes scanned the thinned-out crowd. There were still the die-hard, avid enthusiasts bundled in blankets, sipping hot coffee from the concession stands, or even something stronger to help keep them warm. And then he saw her.

Gripping a camera as if it were part of her very soul, she maneuvered about to get down to the lower level and walk towards the corral of bulls. She shouldn't have even gotten that far. Security should've stopped her immediately, but there she was, strutting around near the pens without a care in the world, focused solely on taking pictures through her camera's lens.

She was about thirty. Pretty with long auburn hair, streaks of copper and red that caught the fading sunlight. Her skin was almost alabaster, and she wasn't overly thin. He didn't care for those women who looked like he needed to force feed them just to get them to look healthy. She was a bit thick around the waistline, but that was what he personally preferred. He watched her as she moved about, trying to get closer to one of the bulls with a speckled white-and-red color. She was so engrossed on the bull she paid no attention to the other animals watching her, including one of the meanest around: a solid black bull named Devil. Why was she blind to the dangers just to get a picture? Where the hell was security?

He glanced back at the arena, trying to see who was up and where security might be in hopes of flagging them down. He was due to ride soon, but was it enough time to go to her? He was about three riders away. Five minutes, maybe ten tops. Chase hopped over the railing he'd been leaning on and jogged over to the pen.

"Hey! Lady! You're not supposed to be back here. You need to go before you get hurt!"

She looked up, startled, and her rich, blue eyes caught him off guard, stealing his breath. She was absolutely stunning. Devil turned when Chase called for her to get away from the metal bars. Stupid female had climbed in between the outer area to the inner walkway. Why didn't she climb into the pen itself and be done with it? She was going to get herself killed and put the entire event in jeopardy. The bull lowered his head before he took off straight for her back. Although his horns had been filed down to rid the sharp points for the safety of the riders, it didn't mean he couldn't cause harm with them. Chase ran towards her, yelling for her to get out immediately. She blushed, a rosy color coming to her pale cheeks, as she realized she'd been caught and slowly leaned down to crawl back through the bars. It was only as she turned sideways did she realize a bull was coming for her.

She squealed and literally fell outside of the inner ring just as Devil reached where she'd been poking through. Security began coming over, as did the handlers of the bulls. They may be just animals to some, but they were sport animals and moneymakers to anyone involved in the sport and therefore were given the utmost care and protection.

Chase reached her first and helped her stand. Within milliseconds they were surrounded by security and others. Everyone was talking and it was total mayhem. Chase couldn't even get close enough to make sure she was alright, having been pushed out of the way.

Brandon, a bullfighter, ambled over to him just as Chase was about to force his way back to the woman's side. "Dude, you're up. Let's go before you're asked to forfeit."

Chase felt torn, wanting to go back to the woman and not wanting to forfeit his opportunity for the event's purse. He couldn't ask Brandon to step in while he was riding, but he was worried what would happen to her if he left her alone. Plus, he didn't want to lose sight of her. Not yet, anyway. At least he wanted her name. True, he couldn't ever be with her. She was human and he…well…wasn't. At least not entirely.

"Yo, Chase! Let's go. Security will keep her for a while just to make sure everything is okay. That should be long enough for you to get your eight seconds in and take a bow. Now go!"

"Yeah. Yeah. Going." Giving the woman, whose hair was the only thing he could see within the crowds that surrounded her, a last look, he headed for the chutes. He needed to focus and put her out of his thoughts for the next few minutes, but he was finding it extremely hard to do so and he didn't fully understand why.

Once he got into the chute she disappeared from his thoughts, as did everything else, including the audience. There was him and the bull, named Scorpion, who he was riding. A brown-and-tan bull, anxious to be let out in order to buck his rider off his back and known for his high kicks. Chase breathed in the scent of the musky animal as he adjusted his glove while climbing onto the animal's back. The odor of Scorpion was strong and helped him focus on the bull between his muscular thighs. He gripped and re-gripped the braid strap, known as the bull rope, until he was comfortably secure with it, then gave a slight nod to indicate he was ready.

The chute gate opened, and Scorpion bucked, reared, kicked, spun and twisted as he tried desperately to get Chase off his back. Chase held tightly to the braided rope while keeping his free hand in the air, sure to not touch either himself or the bull as he mentally counted the eight seconds off in his head. He focused on feeling the animal's muscles contract and relax between his legs as it bucked, using the knowledge to ride the bull as if he were a part of the beast. When he heard the horn indicate the end of his allotted time, he loosened his grip and rolled off Scorpion, landing on all fours before jumping up and running for the wooden fence in order to get out of the way from the still-bucking mammal.

Looking up at the scoreboard, Chase waited for the results. Judge one scored twenty-two for the bull. Judge two scored twenty-six for the bull for a total of forty-eight out of the fifty he could earn. Now, for his personal scores. Judge three scored eighteen. He still needed to get a total of thirty-five points for his half, which means Judge four had to give him a score of seventeen or higher. Could he have screwed it up? A brief moment of doubt fluttered on gossamer wings within his stomach as he waited. Judge four gave him a score of nineteen. He made second place, which still offered a decent-sized purse. Of course, it was all dependent on tomorrow's rides. Anything could happen between now and then. He hopped off the fence and headed back to the bull pens. He could now give his entire focus to the woman who intrigued him.

He noticed the large crowd was still gathered around her. The arguing amongst the stock contractor, security and the woman was becoming overly heated, although Chase understood the reasoning. He, himself, was pretty angry at the unknown woman for putting herself and the animals in danger, maybe even the event itself. If something had happened, it could've done some major damage to the reputation of the event.

This time, Chase forced himself to the center of the group as he tried to quickly assess the situation.

"Look. It's no one's fault. I take full responsibility for getting so close to the bulls. I had no intention of harming them or doing anything to them. I just wanted to get a clear shot of them. I really meant no harm." The woman tried to reason with those around her.

The stock contractor, Manny, shook his head. "Did you check her for anything?"

The security head, Mason, stood with his arms crossed, never taking his eyes off the woman. "We only did a search of her bag. Her ID, a hotel room key, a few bucks and camera equipment is all she has on her."

Chase spoke up. "I saw her. She was solely focused on taking pictures, she paid no attention to the danger she put herself in. I truly believe she had no thought of the jeopardy she put anyone in, especially herself. She was just very intent on getting her picture. Security was nowhere around, so she took advantage of getting close, too close to the bulls. I'm sure she wasn't there to harm them."

Chase's commanding voice broke through to the others standing about.

"That's right. All I wanted was some pictures of the bulls. I wouldn't hurt them. They're magnificent creatures. I just wasn't thinking about anything other than getting closer to them for a better picture without the bars in the way," she strongly reiterated.

"The bars are there to protect you from them as

well as them from you," Manny said, taking his cowboy hat off to run a hand around the rim.

Mason shifted his body from one foot to the other. "What do you want us to do with her?"

Everyone turned their attention to Manny, knowing he'd have the final say since the animals were his.

Putting his hat back on, Manny shook his head. "Get her out of here. Let her take her pictures from the stands like everyone else if she wants, but get those guards back over here to protect my stock and keep a watch on her until she leaves, or anyone else who gets it into their head to visit my herd up close and personal. If she comes back tomorrow night, make sure she only has access to the stands and nothing more." Manny turned his back on all of them, proceeding to his stock, feeling the need to check on each one personally. Although the bulls will only perform once a night, he wanted to be sure they were all okay.

Mason was about to grab the woman and lead her roughly back out of the area, but Chase blocked him. "I'll escort her."

She looked up at Chase and again, his breath caught in his throat due to her enticing blue eyes staring at him. He lightly gripped her elbow and led her through the small group that had gathered around them as he made his way towards the stands.

"Thank you. I have a feeling had you not said something in my defense, it might've been worse for me."

Chase stopped and pulled her around to face him, his features growing dark with anger. "You're lucky it wasn't worse for you before any of us arrived. Devil was about to skewer you like a shish-kabob. You should've never been anywhere near those pens."

"I know. I said I was sorry. And I am."

Taking a couple of deep breaths to calm himself, he let himself relax his grip slightly, but still refused to let her go entirely. "What's your name?"

"Aurora. Aurora Taylor." She looked him over, noticing he still hadn't released her. He was tall and she could tell he was a Native American. His shoulder-length, silky black hair stuck out from under the black cowboy hat he wore tilted over his eyes. And his eyes, they were amazing. The most unique color she'd ever seen. A light golden amber that almost seemed to shine from within. His skin was darkened from the sun, and he was muscular with broad shoulders, bulging biceps and thick thighs. He still wore only one glove for riding. She found him extremely handsome, blushing lightly with the thought of how good looking he was and the naughty thoughts that immediately followed as a result. "Thank you again for helping me, not only with the crowd, but calling to me when the bull began to charge."

Chase nodded, then he noticed she started shivering. He could sense it wasn't from the cold air but probably from the shock over what transpired suddenly hitting her full force. "Come on. I'll buy you a drink and you can tell me why you were so intent on getting a picture of a bull that it was worth risking your life for."

"Suddenly, I feel like I could use one. Normally, I'm not much of a drinker."

"I think you're starting to realize the direness of the situation and what almost happened. A drink will help calm you."

"I should be buying you the drink for helping me."

"You can buy the next one."

She gave him a look of surprise before quickly recovering. "Deal."

Chase smiled and led her through the area under the stadium seats, which were lined with vendors and food booths. At the end of the row was a makeshift bar. "What'll you have?"

She looked over the choices. Aurora detested beer and the wine would probably be mediocre. Her shivering was becoming more pronounced, so something strong seemed the way to go. "Rum and Diet Coke."

Chase nodded, then ordered a whiskey for himself. Pulling out his worn leather wallet, he paid for the drinks, then led them both to a picnic table nearby. Sheltered from the wind, it enabled them to have some quiet time, since most of the crowd had already left for the night or were not interested in food or beverages at this time, as it was close to the end of the event.

"Thank you…" Aurora blushed again. "I'm sorry. I didn't catch your name."

Chase chuckled. "I guess I didn't give it. Chase White Bear at your service, ma'am." He tapped the tip of his hat slightly before picking up his shot of whiskey. Normally he'd down it in one gulp, but he didn't want their time to end so soon, so he took a small sip, returning the glass to the table.

"Well, thank you Chase White Bear." Aurora used the stirrer to mix up her drink, then took a sip, feeling the warmth go down her throat leading its way into her belly.

"You were about to tell me about the importance of those pictures?"

She chuckled. "I'm not sure importance is the correct word. I'm an opportunist. They were there so proud, strong and intriguing. As I'd never seen one so close, I just couldn't resist in taking their picture and capturing the moment. I'm afraid I got extremely engrossed to the point I lost awareness to everything else around me."

"What do you do with the pictures? Are you a photojournalist or something?"

"Something. I sell the really good pictures to magazines to use for their articles. I also display some at an art gallery I own. These were mostly going to be just for me, unless I saw something I thought would appeal to the public. Most are just for my personal use." She took a couple of swallows from her drink, hoping the alcohol would alleviate her shaking, which she knew came from delayed shock over almost being severely or even mortally injured.

"You own your own gallery? Where?" Chase noticed she was still shaking, albeit not as badly, so he reached out to hold her hand comfortingly.

Aurora glanced down at his hand covering hers. He was such a large man; it made hers look like a child's compared to his. She wondered what he'd be like with children of his own, though where that thought came from dismayed her. In her mind's eye, she saw him sitting on the ground in a meadow as one child sat in his lap while two others ran circles around him. He would laugh at their antics. Then the children morphed into animals and Chase laughed harder at them. Aurora blinked and downed the rest of her drink. She'd had flashes before in her life, but nothing so strong or vivid. But was her vision one of the past, present or future, and why it would matter was beyond her. She was pretty positive she wasn't his type. Mostly because she didn't think she was anyone's type, but especially a man this handsome.

"Are you okay?" His voice held a concern for her.

Chase noticed she had paled and seemed to blank out for a moment, only to shake a bit more strongly moments later before she reached out to finish her drink in a few quick gulps. "Do you want another drink?"

Aurora nodded. "Yes. But, I think it's my turn

to get this round." She pulled her hand away, got up and headed to the concession stand. She hated those flashes of clarity or imagination or premonition? And worse, she detested those flickers of reality, whether imagined or not from her own inadequacies. She may not be model thin, but she was smart, caring and even somewhat pretty.

Chase frowned as he watched her depart so rapidly, her heels clicking along the wooden planks before she reached the gravel. Something happened but he wasn't sure what had changed her mood.

"Two shots of whiskey and a rum and Diet Coke, please."

When the drinks were brought up, Aurora took one of the whiskey shots and downed it, handing the surprised woman back the now empty glass. "Thanks."

It was the boost she needed to get out of her own self-depreciating head. She had a lot to offer any man she wanted once she got past her own self-doubt. She grabbed the other two beverages and headed back to the table where Chase was waiting for her.

He'd finished his shot by the time she returned. Smiling, she set his new shot down in front of him while feeling the whiskey she'd just had herself work its warmth down her body. Almost immediately her shaking had abated significantly.

"Are you okay?" He repeated the question he'd asked before she swiftly departed.

"Yes. Sorry about that. I am."

"I didn't mean to get too personal with my question. Sorry if I was being too forward."

"No. No. You were fine. I just… Sorry. It's nothing to do with you or your questions. In answer, my gallery is in St. Louis."

"What brought you to Deadwood? Surely it wasn't to be harassing the bulls," he teased lightly, a lopsided grin on his lips.

Aurora laughed at his banter. She was finding him very easy to talk to, and although she didn't want the evening to end, she knew it would. The event was over for the evening; the concessions were closing up almost as soon as she purchased the drinks. People were starting to leave, yet Chase didn't seem to be paying attention to anything other than the two of them. She couldn't remember the last time she was the sole focus of someone seemingly interested in her, making her feel important and special. "Business, but I decided to add a bit of a vacation around it. I've never been in South Dakota before and Deadwood seemed a good point to venture forth exploring."

"Business?"

"Yes. I'm volunteering my work for the Wild Horse Sanctuary to prepare a calendar for them to sell in order to help raise money for their altruistic efforts. I'm hoping to get enough pictures for the next two or three years' worth of calendars. While I'm here, I also want to explore the Cave of the Winds, Mt. Rushmore, Crazy Horse Monument, maybe even do the 1880's train ride between Hill City and Keystone. There seems to be so much to see and do here. Where are you from?"

"Not far. I live near the Pine Ridge Reservation most of the time." He downed his shot in one gulp this time, not savoring it like before. "We'd best go before Mason gets upset we're still hanging around. Can I walk you to your car?"

"I actually took the trolley here."

"Then, may I drive you wherever you're going to?"

Quickly finishing her drink, she nodded. "I'd like that." She smiled as she stood, noticing her shaking was replaced with a multitude of butterflies in her stomach.

Chase followed suit and led her to the back lot where his Ford F150 red truck was parked. He opened the door for her, then shut it before he walked around to get in on the driver's side. Once they were both buckled up, he started the engine. "Where to?"

"I'm staying at the Franklin. Do you travel to other rodeos?"

"You mean PBR events? Yes, I try and enter several throughout the year."

"What got you into bull riding?"

He shrugged as he pulled out of the parking lot.

"I like the thrill and the danger. The money isn't bad either."

"I assume you're Lakota if you live near Pine Ridge?"

"Oglala. We're just one of seven bands of the Lakota. It means 'They Scatter Their Own.'"

"What are the other six?"

"There is the Sichangu, also known as the Brule, which means 'Burned Thighs.' The Itazipcho or Sans Arc, meaning 'Without Bows.' The Hunkpapa, which means 'Camps at the End of the Camp Circle.' The Mnikowozu or Miniconjou, meaning 'Planters by the Water.' The Sihasapa, 'Blackfeet,' and finally the Oohenunpa, which means 'Two Kettles.' Then, there's also the Nakota and the Dakota who were once all part of our tribe before the split centuries ago. The difference in our languages is the L versus the N or D, respectively."

"I'm not sure I understand."

"Friends in Lakota is kola, but in Nakota language it's kona, and in Dakota language it'd be koda. But we are all Sioux, named that by the

French when they first met us. They named us Nadouessioux when our enemies, the Ojibwas, told them that's what we're called. It was actually the name they gave us. Na Dou Esse, which means snakelike ones or enemies. The French spelled it N-A-D-O-U-S-S-I-O-U-X and the English shortened it to just Sioux. We prefer either the band name, Lakota, or the sub-band name, which for me it'd be Oglala."

"Fascinating. I never really knew any of this, but then history was never my forte. Or Native current events. I'm sorry to say there are not many Natives in St. Louis, and we just don't learn much about the differences in school. Which is a tragedy. We really should. I'd love to learn more."

Chase pulled up across the street from the historic Franklin Hotel, looking forlornly at the building for a moment before he turned his attention to her. "I'd love the opportunity. I've not eaten yet. I know it's late, but it's best not to eat before riding a bull. Would you care to join me for a late dinner?"

Aurora was relieved. She wasn't quite willing

to say goodbye to him just yet either. She might never see him after the event tomorrow night. He'd go back to his home and prepare for another event or whatever it was he did. Giving him a genuine enthusiastic smile, she nodded. "I'd love to. And maybe you will tell me more?"

"Sure. Anything you want to know." Chase pulled away from the Franklin and continued down the street. "How is Mustang Sally's?"

"Sounds good. I've heard they have wonderful burgers."

"Shakes are good too, and they also have drinks. We could go to one of the saloons if you'd prefer, or if you want something special, something else."

"No. I'm really not much of a drinker. I think I had my limit for the month. Mustang Sally's is fine."

He found a parking space rather quickly, hopping out of the vehicle to open her door and help her out. It was still far too cold to sit outside, so they were both grateful for the heated warmth when they entered the building and found a seat.

There were only a handful of people inside, but then again it was rather late when they decided to do dinner. Most everyone was probably warming themselves up with drinks in the multitude of bars and casinos along Main Street.

After placing their order, Aurora looked around the room, suddenly feeling a bit uneasy. She thought Chase was way too handsome to be with the likes of her, and in the moments after the waitress departed to put in their order, she was a bit unsure of herself.

Chase sensed her unease, though unsure what brought it about. He cleared his throat. "Have you had a chance to see much of South Dakota?"

She shook her head. "No. I just got here earlier today and mostly got settled in. I saw the advertisements for the PBR and, having never seen one before, thought I would check it out. My goodness! It was very…invigorating. I honestly don't know how you all do what you do."

"Like anything else, we all have our own

personal stories. But this is a sport to almost all of us in it. A sport between man and beast."

"Are the animals ever hurt?"

"No. Most who don't understand the sport don't know that the bulls, like men, are born to it. It's what they want to do. Not something we make them do. And they are prized, given the best of everything. They only work once per event. We draw to see who we get to ride from the animals that are selected to participate that day. They get their own set of scores, combined with our set of scores to make up the final scores we get. Which, of course, determines the winner."

"It sounds more humane than I originally thought. It's good to know. I would've hated to know those magnificent beasts were being abused or mistreated in any way."

"It's why Manny was so concerned over you being so close to them. Don't get me wrong. He would've eventually worried about you, but he is focused on making sure his bulls are okay. What sights, other than the PBR, are you planning on while you are here?"

"There is far more than I originally thought, from all the brochures I've picked up since my arrival. I guess the standard Mt. Rushmore, and visiting Keystone. Honestly, there is just so many choices, I'm not really sure. I only have two days. Sunday is my appointment to take the photos at the sanctuary. Monday is in case I've missed anything, and I head home Tuesday."

"Tell you what, why don't I take you sightseeing tomorrow afternoon and then you can join me in the evening for the final competition. Maybe we can do dinner afterwards again, like tonight?" Chase's tone was deep, hopeful.

Before she could answer, the waitress returned with their food. Chase waited for her to give him an answer, a concern she would say no.

After she commented on the deliciousness of the burger, as well as the size of it, she set it aside to wipe her hands. "I would hate to interfere in your plans or anything." That self-doubt of not being good enough for someone so handsome jumped into her mind and plagued her with those tendrils of disquiet.

He reached across and placed his hand over hers. "I have no plans for tomorrow. I would be honored to show you around."

How could she say no to that? The sincerity in his voice, his warm hand covering hers and his overall persuasion swept away any skepticism she had. She smiled and nodded. "I'd love it. Thank you for the offer." After all, who wouldn't want to spend more time with a man who looked like a warrior god, making her heart melt with each smile?

By the time their meal was finished, they made plans to sightsee for the next day and she planned on attending the following evening's PBR final event as his guest to make sure she wasn't causing any problems while at the arena. Although the rain had subsided and the wind died down, it was still chilly. Since they both had coats on and he wasn't ready to bid her goodnight just yet, he offered to walk her back to the Franklin. It was only a couple of blocks from Mustang Sally's and would give him more time to spend with her. He used the excuse of the slight chill still in the air to wrap his arm around her shoulders and press her against his body for warmth.

At the hotel, she climbed the first couple of steps, then turned back to face him. "Thank you for such a pleasant evening. I truly am sorry I caused so much trouble earlier."

"You're welcome. I'm just glad you're okay. Things could've been so much worse."

"It's all because of you that I am." She was level to him, standing two steps higher than he was. She reached out and cupped his cheek, her thumb caressing his lips. She couldn't stop herself, leaning in to kiss him. She didn't worry if he'd find her too forward or not be interested, but he didn't pull away in disgust as part of her expected him to. Instead, he gripped her hips and jerked her closer to him. One hand slipped up her back to grip her head as he thrust his tongue between her lips, delving and exploring the recesses of her mouth. Tasting her. She moaned softly under his advances. The cold air did nothing to alleviate the heat quickly rising within her belly and spreading throughout her body.

She was surprised and disappointed when he pulled back from her. He still gripped her to hold her steady before slowly relaxing his clasp on her.

"You better get inside before you get sick." His voice was deeper than before, full of a lustful desire, his eyes dark.

"I guess I probably should." Although free from his embrace, she hadn't moved.

"Well. Good night, then. I'll see you tomorrow about 11 to visit Crazy Horse Monument." Without another word, he left her and walked swiftly down the street towards Mustang Sally's and his truck without even a backwards glance.

She stood on the stairs of the Franklin bewildered as she watched him disappear down the street.

"What's wrong with him?"

The voice startled Aurora and she turned, only then noticing a young petite woman sitting in the rocking chair in the corner of the porch.

"Sorry?" Aurora had enough surprises in one evening; she didn't need to be spooked by some nosy onlooker.

"I'm just saying, I don't think I've seen a man move away from such an open invitation as he just did. I apologize. I tend to be a bit nosy and forthcoming. Too much for my own good, I've been told." She gave Aurora a sweet smile, setting Aurora more at ease.

Aurora turned back towards Chase's retreating back and shrugged. "Not really sure. Could be me." There was that self-doubt again.

"He's a fool, then. By the way, name's Allison. I'm from Bismarck. Didn't I see him in the rodeo?"

Aurora smirked. "I'm Aurora. Yeah, he was one of the riders today."

"Moving up in rank, I noticed. He's got a good shot for the lead, depending on his ride tomorrow."

"Oh?" Aurora's interest piqued and she moved closer to Allison. Putting her back to Chase and hopefully getting him out of her mind in the process, she gave Allison her full attention. "You follow the riders?"

"Kind of. I actually just like watching cowboys in general. I never miss the one in Deadwood. It's only a couple of hours drive from where I live and a chance to relax and stare without being unseemly."

Chuckling, Aurora nodded in agreement. "I admit they are a pleasure to watch."

"I admit it's probably stupid. It's not like there aren't any in Bismarck. But watching them with a bull between their legs and all that bucking action, well, it just makes me swoon. How can a woman not be excited over that? How can a woman not be in love with a cowboy? They are just so…swoonworthy."

"I hadn't really given it much thought, but I guess you're right. There is certainly something about a cowboy." *Especially one like Chase,* she added silently.

Allison stood and moved to the lobby entrance. "Think I'll call it a night. It was nice meeting you, Aurora. Hope I see you around."

"Likewise." Aurora watched her enter, then

after a few moments of looking forlornly down Main Street, she sighed and headed to her room.

Chapter Two

Aurora looked in the mirror as she brushed her hair, her hands shaking slightly. Thank goodness for makeup, as she'd gotten very little sleep and the dark circles under her eyes were the result, she was grateful she could hide with cosmetics. Although she'd been exhausted, she couldn't seem to shut her brain off long enough to get any real sleep. And what little she did get was laced with nightmares she couldn't quiet remember. Bits and pieces of Deadwood as it probably looked over a hundred years ago, with prospectors wandering down Main Street to the calls of painted ladies from the balconies and windows of the saloons. She remembered she found the sight disgusting and her heart raced from fear of being associated with such a deplorable profession. She tried to run away, but she felt something was chasing her, although she wasn't sure what it could be. The wind had turned cold as leaves blew across her path. There was nowhere safe she could run to, nowhere she could hide, even though she wasn't sure what she was trying to run from.

Out of breath, she tripped over a chair and realized she was in the hotel's hallway. Suddenly, she was grateful she wasn't one to sleep in the nude, as she had to head down to the lobby and get another key to get back into her sleeping quarters. Sleepwalking was something she didn't think she'd ever done in the past. She could only assume it had to do with the day's activities and her subconscious trying to make sense of it all. But then again, it might have to do with her own special gifts. She'd seen Chase surrounded by children in an open field and knew from their conversation he was neither married nor a father. Was this a vision of the past or simply her intuitive thoughts processing the historical décor of the Franklin and Deadwood? Could it even have been a premonition of his future yet to come? If so, she was glad he was happy, but the rest didn't make any sense. Why would the children change into various animals? Were they representing the characteristics of those creatures? Thinking about it only gave her a headache.

Once she was safely tucked back in her bed, her mind wouldn't settle down enough as she continued to think about Chase and his response to her kiss. He appeared to like her, seemed to want to be with her, buying her drinks, going out for a late supper, walking her back to her hotel and planning on taking her sightseeing today. Their conversation throughout the evening was easy going and pleasant. Yet, he pulled away when she kissed him. At first she thought he would come up to her room, especially after the initial way he responded, but he thrust her from him and couldn't seem to get away from her fast enough. What had she done to cause him to change his mind? Would he even show today, or would he stand her up? Did she read more into his kindness as interest when he was only trying to be helpful and protective?

She'd always been one to go after what she wanted, as witnessed when she got too close to the bull pens last night. Maybe he didn't care for a woman who could protect herself or make the first move? Maybe he felt too manly to allow her to kiss him first? Or maybe she was a horrible kisser? Maybe she assumed he was free, and he actually wasn't, despite him not wearing a wedding ring or telling her otherwise.

"Ugh." Aurora admonished herself, throwing her brush onto the bureau and turning to look through the windows to see if he was approaching for the umpteenth time.

Her room was a fabulous corner room overlooking Main Street. The furniture was made to look antique, although she knew they were modern replicas.

Still, she didn't see a red pickup truck anywhere. It was almost eleven, but she was beginning to despair of seeing him again, positive she scared him off. It made her wonder about attending the PBR tonight for the final rounds of competition. If she went and he saw her, he'd think she was stalking him. She could go and stay in the back, out of sight, but that wasn't a guarantee of them not running into each other even by accident.

She glanced down at her phone. Eleven-fifteen

am. No sign of his truck. Her heart fell. She'd really enjoyed spending time with him and was excited about seeing him again. Leave it to her to ruin it. Or maybe he really was just being nice to her and didn't have any real interest in her. She probably blew his kindness way out of proportion within her own mind.

Aurora resigned herself to being stood up when she heard a knock at her door. Trepidation caused her to check on her guest, assuming it was someone from the hotel staff, probably the maid wanting to get in and clean the room. She didn't get her hopes up that it was Chase. Not again.

Opening the door, her heart skipped a beat. There he was in all his handsome cowboy glory holding a bouquet of sunflowers out to her.

He touched the tip of his black hat. "Morning, ma'am. Did you sleep well?"

Aurora took the proffered flowers. "Morning, sir. Thank you. They're beautiful." She wasn't one to lie, so felt it best to ignore the last question. He didn't need to know how anxious and restless she'd been all night long.

"Chase, please."

"Aurora, then. If you're formal with ma'am, then I'll respond equally so, with sir."

He laughed. "Fair enough, Aurora."

Oh, how she loved the way he said her name with that deep voice and slight twang. "Please come in while I see if I can find something to put these in." She held the door wider to allow him to pass into the room.

"I'm sorry. I didn't even think of that."

"It's fine. I'll use my water container and be on the lookout for another while we're exploring. It'll give me a reason to buy a new souvenir. Besides, sunflowers are my favorite. I want to make sure they last for a while. It was very thoughtful of you."

She dumped the ice from her water bottle and refilled the container with cool water before placing the flowers in.

"They're mine too. My mother used to tell me you couldn't look at one and not smile. And I'm fascinated with the way they follow the sun." He watched her put them in the corner between the two windows to be sure they got plenty of light. "Besides, I made you wait, so I needed a good apology."

"Apology accepted." She giggled softly.

Her movements were a bit stiff and he could smell the heavy makeup she wore despite her face looking natural. With his spirit guide's abilities, he knew she hadn't slept well at all, but then, neither had he.

"Are you ready for our adventure today?"

Aurora made sure the flowers wouldn't tip over as she nodded. "I'm ready."

"Great. Let's go." He opened the door for her and waited for her to grab her purse, camera bag and hat before he followed her, pulling the wooden door closed behind them. He couldn't help but look around. The building was very old and his animal inside was prancing nervously at knowing what still remained. Chase led her down a side corridor towards the back of the hotel where his truck was parked.

Aurora hadn't known that was there, but it explained why she hadn't seen him arrive. She didn't understand him. He was such a conundrum to her. Last night he seemed as if he couldn't get away from her fast enough when she tried to kiss him and today he seemed as if he were courting her. Was he old fashioned? Did he prefer being the macho man and needed to make the first move? She knew women could be off-standish, but she never heard of a man preferring to wait when a woman was offering herself up on a silver platter. Or did he think she was just playing him? Or after him for his bull riding fame? Did he think she was some kind of groupie?

He climbed into the truck after he made sure she was secure on the passenger side, soon heading in the opposite direction from which Aurora drove into town.

She knew this road led to Hill City, Keystone, Mt. Rushmore and Crazy Horse Monument. Aurora had investigated the route as a way for her to also get to the Wild Horse Sanctuary for the photo shoot.

Her reverie was broken when he quietly spoke.

"Will you be attending the event tonight?"

"I thought about it, but I wasn't sure if it'd be a problem or not. After last night's debacle and all." There, the white elephant in the truck was officially out.

Chase reached over and gripped her hand giving it a slight squeeze. "Please come. I'd like you there."

So much for any explanation. She thought her concern was clear, but obviously it wasn't and she decided it wasn't worth arguing about. "How can I refuse such a request?"

"Great. I'll let a friend of mine, Brandon, who's one of the bullfighters, meet you and take you to a special seating area. It's a friends and family section. It'll be the first time I'll make use of it." He cast a sideways glance to catch her expression over his last statement.

"In other words, this is your way of making sure I'm not getting in trouble by going places where I shouldn't?" she teased, though it hadn't escaped her notice about not bringing any family or friends to the reserved section or that he avoided the debacle comment.

"Well, maybe," he teased back, giving her a lopsided cocky smile. He followed the signs that led to Mt. Rushmore.

"Take your camera out. The heads will be framed by the tunnel blasted through this mountain in just a minute. Although I don't appreciate the heads being here or what they stand for, I do admit it is a sight to behold."

Aurora followed his instructions and prepped her camera for several shots of the monumental heads as they appeared surrounded by the mountain made for the road's access. He pulled over to the scenic point lookout once they got through the tunnel.

"This is about as good a view as any, I guess." He put the truck in park and hopped out to open her door.

He stood by his vehicle and watched her. Her hair sparkled and glistened with the sun's rays hitting the copper notes. She wasn't overly thin, but he appreciated that. Actually, she was what many would consider fat, but he found her fluffy shape enticing. She was smaller than him, but still tall for a woman. About five feet nine inches, which also suited his six foot four frame. He was beguiled by her from the first moment he saw her by the bull pens. He couldn't stop staring at her, though the beast inside him paced anxiously wanting to take her, something he couldn't allow.

She snapped a few more pictures, then changed the lens for close-ups of each head. It didn't escape her notice that he didn't look at the monument but kept his focus on her. She put on a couple of special effects filters and snapped a few more photos. Somehow, she felt guilty making him wait. Something else he said also bothered her.

Getting plenty of shots, she headed back towards him, putting her camera back into the bag. However, she stopped him from opening the truck door by placing her hand on his. "Can we talk for a moment? Without the distraction of driving?"

His eyebrow shot up as he wondered what she had to say that was so important as to do it on the side of the road, even if it was a turnoff. "Sure." He looked around, then pointed to a path on the left. "We can walk there. It leads to a little picnic table. Very few know it's here, so we can speak freely."

"It's not that dire. I just wanted you to focus on the conversation and not the curves."

He eyes slowly went down and then up her body as he cocked a lopsided smirk. "I'd rather focus on your curves."

Her whole body tingled, her knees becoming instantly weak. She had meant the curvy road, but his insinuation made her want to swoon. How could he do that so easily with just a look and a drop in tone to his rich voice?

Chase realized his meaning was not totally lost on her and she was discombobulated by his comment. "Still, this is a bit more private and we can take our time with the conversation." He turned, shifting his pants slightly and taking some calming breaths to settle his beast down.

She nodded and waited until he locked up the truck, then followed him down the path. It was small, narrow, and she had to watch her step closely. She tripped on a root, but he caught her and held her steady. When he was sure she was alright, they continued the rest of the way. In a short distance, the path opened up to a small clearing with a picnic table in the center and a small fire pit nearby.

Chase sat on the edge of the table, one foot planted firmly on the ground and the other dangling slightly. He tipped his hat back and tilted his head as he waited for her to speak.

Aurora was nervous. There were so many things she wanted to know, but she didn't want to offend him in any way. She already felt as if she walked on eggshells with him in some cases as it was; a result of that kiss. She debated on asking him about last night, but she was scared of his answer. And confused as to his response after his comment about her curves just minutes ago. She didn't remember being so perplexed by a man as she was

Chase. One moment he seemed to really be into her and the next, not so much. It was really beginning to drive her crazy, especially with her lack of sleep.

When she didn't immediately speak up, he cleared his throat. "You wanted to talk?"

"Well." She looked around the area before she steeled herself to gaze at him. "Please don't take this the wrong way. I'll admit right off the bat I'm ignorant about your situation."

"My situation? What do you mean?"

"Okay. I'm going to just come out and ask, but please realize I want to know. And I'm not meaning to insult you in any way, but I also don't want to make any cultural mistakes."

Chase pulled his leg up onto the bench of the table resting his elbow on his bent knee. He realized she would ask in her own time. "I promise not to be insulted by anything you ask, and I'll tell you the truth as best as I can."

With his assurances, she felt more comfortable to proceed, but not with her concerns about last night. Not yet. Although that was her original reason for wanting to talk to him without distractions, she didn't, quickly having lost her nerve. Instead, she'd ask him about something else she was strongly curious about. "You mentioned earlier you didn't appreciate the heads of Mt. Rushmore being there. I was wondering why? And is it a particular head in general or all of them in their entirety? Is it because of who they represent or something else?"

He frowned, anger seething inside of him over the ignorance of her questions. But he promised her and he knew she was just trying to understand, something many didn't even bother doing. He appreciated her curiosity and was grateful she asked him instead of ignoring the Lakota plight. Although he lived through the government stealing the Black Hills area from his people, sadly he'd learned many Americans today didn't get the Lakota's viewpoint. It wasn't as if it was taught in schools around the country. The government was perfectly happy to forget about the Native people and the land they stole from those who were here first, caring neither for their traditions, language, culture and especially their history, religious or otherwise.

"This is Lakota territory. That mountain with the heads on it is sacred to us. We know it as Six Grandfathers. But, because gold was discovered in our mountains, a treaty promised to us in 1871 was broken. Whites moved in, caring nothing for my people or our sacred lands.

"Without our permission, they hired a Ku Klux Klan leader to sculpt a monument, which originally was supposed to be of those who explored the west and of Red Cloud when the original idea was proposed. Borglum changed the project to those you see today. Those who had no care or interest in our Native culture or our sacred lands." He took his hat off, clutching it in his hands. "And who they chose, it just added insult to injury. George Washington had Native Americans killed in New England. Both he and Thomas Jefferson owned slaves. Jefferson made the Louisiana Purchase, which stole so much land from our kind and instituted the beginnings of the westward relocation of tribes east of the

Mississippi to the west, displacing them off their ancestral lands as well as forcing them to share with other tribes, some of which were enemies of each other before the whites even came to this part of the world. Theodore Roosevelt stated the only good Indian was a dead one. And Abraham Lincoln? He executed thirty-eight Native Americans for theft by public hanging, ignoring the fact food was being withheld by the Indian agents and the Sioux were on the brink of starvation. They had no choice but to steal food in order to survive, but those caught were punished to the extreme to quote, 'set an example.' Then, Borglum took a place holy to us and carved these atrocities. That's equivalent to me going into your church and defacing your altar."

During his speech, Aurora's mouth fell open wider and wider in astonishment. "I honestly didn't know. I didn't understand. I thought reparations were being made for the land and everything else the government took from your people. I didn't know anything about Borglum being a KKK member or the rest of the history of the presidents."

She moved closer to him, meeting him eye to eye. "I can truly understand your distaste. I'm very sorry I brought up such a horrific ordeal you and all the others are going through. Have been through. Thank you for explaining it to me." She was incredulous over what he relayed to her. It was almost too unbelievable. Anger bubbled inside her at the mere thought of what his people must've gone through so many years ago.

"The government tried. They gave the Lakota a couple hundred thousand dollars to make up for the loss of our lands, but we refuse to take it. Our lands are not for sale. They never will be. I've heard the money is being kept in a trust for us and has grown to over a billion dollars with the interest, but we'll never accept it. We won't sell out our grandfathers or our history. There's no price that can be met. We want our land back. Nothing else will suffice."

His words were tinged with a bit of anger and pride, and although she wasn't Lakota, she felt their disgust and dissatisfaction with government treatment of their tribe and their lands. She knew she'd never look at those heads again in the same way she'd done only fifteen minutes ago.

"I wish I had the power to give it back to you and your people. I've always hated the way Indians were treated in the past and how it hadn't really improved in the present. I won't ask to see Mt. Rushmore again, knowing what you've told me. They will never have the same awe-inspiring aspect as they had when I first saw them just moments ago."

Chase reached out and pulled her closer, his legs brushing the outside of her thighs. "I'm glad you asked. I'm glad you wanted to know. Most folks don't care one way or the other, feeling what's done is done and we should move on. But my people are not like that. We can't forget the past or what was done to us in order to steal our lands."

He took a long callused fore-finger and gently traced her jaw line. He dropped his head seemingly about to kiss her when a call from a nearby crow broke the mood and he pulled back. He scanned the trees, his eyes narrowing. "We should head back.

Why don't you start back up the trail? Here's the keys to the truck. I'll be up in a minute." He noticed her quizzical look and answered her unspoken question. "I need to use the facilities. I'll follow in a moment."

Aurora nodded, blushing slightly at his implication as she hastily retreated to give him some privacy.

Chase watched her go until she was out of his line of sight. He turned around to face three men and a woman. The woman was standing just in front of the men, her gray hair braided and hanging down her left side. She approached him. Her petite small frame didn't indicate her severely advanced age. She didn't say anything. She didn't have to.

"I know." Chase took his hat off to show his respect to the elderly woman. "I'm aware she's human."

The taller of the three men took a step forward, folding his arms over his chest.

Chase peered at his steely grey eyes. "I didn't. I know I can't be with her at all. Why are you so worried about this one, when I've been with other human women before?"

The second older male tilted his head and moved to stand next to the woman. "You know we do not normally interfere in your personal affairs. You've done well in keeping outsiders away from finding out about us. About what we really are. However, Zonta doesn't get a good feeling from the one you've chosen to be with today. We've not interceded in your previous liaisons because Zonta didn't fear them. It is best not to get too involved with this one."

Chase's jaw worked silently. He was used to being on his own a bit more than the rest of his band. He'd never before been forewarned about being with anyone. If anything, Zonta and the elders want him to marry and return to the spirit walkers of his band. So what was it about Aurora that frightened them enough to personally come with a warning? "I'm just showing her around before the PBR finals tonight. I'm leaving Deadwood tomorrow to help prepare for the gathering on

Monday. She is aware I'll no longer be around."

"The temptation of her being close won't entice you?" Zonta asked quietly.

"I can't let it. I promised to help set up the area since I was given permission to partake a couple of years on the PBR circuit. I won't break my promise and I won't have a one-night stand with her."

"That is my concern." Zonta gave him an unblinking stare.

Chase blinked. Now he was even more confused. Why should Zonta care whether or not he had a one-night stand with a human?

The male next to Zonta folded his arms across his chest. "We trust you."

Zonta nodded. "Then we've nothing else to discuss. We trust you. I—trust you."

Chase gave Zonta a lopsided smile. "I should get back to showing her around. I won't forget what you advised."

He turned, jogging back up the path towards Aurora and his truck. Zonta shook her head. Mahkah unfolded his arms and looked at his three companions. Mato sighed while Kyle remained quiet. They could tell from Zonta's expression she was still concerned.

Mato stepped forward. "Will she bring trouble upon us?"

"She'll bring something he won't expect. None of us will. It's not her fault. She means us no harm, but something follows her, and whatever it is, that is what's out to destroy us all."

"He won't heed the warning?" Mahkah crossed his arms again.

"I don't think so. But maybe, for once, he will listen to us and not consummate their friendship. If he does become intimate, we will all pay the price."

"Should we have demanded it of him? Gave him a stronger warning?" Mato's eyes peered towards the path Chase had just departed on.

Zonta shook her head. "I don't think anything else we could say would've made any further impact on him then us coming to see him personally as we've done." She sighed. "Kyle, keep an eye on her. Brandon can continue to watch Chase. I fear that's the best we can do at this time. In the interim, let us go. We've many guests coming soon for which we must prepare." Without another word, she shifted, her arms spread out, covering themselves in feathers. Once she turned into a crow, she spread her wings and took off.

Mato shifted into a magpie and followed her while Mahkah shifted into a bighorn sheep to follow on the ground as the others glided through the air. Kyle remained standing in the clearing for a few more minutes. He had other plans, plans that were not totally being interfered with by having been assigned to watching the female of Chase's interest. Somehow, he'd work around the few problems that might otherwise arise . Somehow, he'd complete what he needed to do. Licking his lips, he swiftly shifted into an oriel and took off to Crazy Horse Monument where he knew they were going. Best to beat them there, he thought as he took flight.

Chapter Three

Chase pulled into Crazy Horse Monument's parking lot. "We should be in time for some of the cultural dances."

"Perfect. I noticed there's a tour to get closer to the carving itself. It's absolutely huge."

Chase nodded. "All four of those heads at Mt. Rushmore can fit on the arm of Crazy Horse. The heads of the presidents are sixty feet high, whereas the arm of Crazy Horse is 87 feet high. The arm is two hundred sixty-three feet long, whereas the heads are only about one hundred ninety to two hundred feet long. It's also privately funded. There will never be government assistance to help finish this project so it's taking longer than many expect."

He paid for her admittance and for himself. He knew the money went to helping the monument and he had no qualms about paying. "Are you getting hungry? The Laughing River Restaurant has excellent food."

"Actually, yes, I am. I'll bow to your wisdom on the subject. The restaurant sounds perfect."

"Have you ever had an Indian taco?"

"No. What's that?"

"It's Indian fry bread with meat, lettuce, tomato, cheese, olives and sour cream on top."

"That sounds delicious. I'm in."

"Good. Let's go eat first and then we can explore without my stomach interfering loudly over the other commentary we might want to listen to."

Aurora laughed as she let him lead her through the main building across the courtyard and to the restaurant, which had a spectacular view of Crazy Horse. Once seated, she looked over the menu, though she was pretty certain sitting down she was going to order the Indian taco and, truthfully, nothing else looked as good, except maybe the buffalo burger, which she could pretty much get anywhere else. Chase recommended the taco, so that's what she'd have. She'd given up asking him about leaving so abruptly the night before. She decided it wasn't worth the chance of them not enjoying the afternoon together, albeit, the whole event still plagued her slightly. However, she was grateful for the warmer weather today as opposed to the bitter cold of last night.

After lunch, they headed out to the square to listen and watch some of the dancers in costumed dress, then walked around several other exhibits. Aurora was glad cameras had gone digital, because if she had to use film, she'd probably have run out ages ago. As it was, she had to change the SD card, having already filled one up.

"The dancers talk about their names and being given six of them. Do you have more than Chase?"

"Yes. My birth name is different. It's Chatan, which means hawk. But Chase was easier for others to say. We also have nicknames, honor names, secret names, spirit names and special deeds names, but the last two are only know to the Medicine men and each particular individual. Many of us go by our nicknames instead of our birth names. It's easier for most folk. The majority of the elders prefer their birth names, while us younger tribal members like our nicknames over our birth ones, especially in today's day and age. Personally, I like Chase, and it's close enough to Chatan."

They ended up in the gift shop. Aurora wasn't one for trivial trinkets, but she did need to get a new water bottle and found one that was insulated she really liked. She also looked at the multitude of books. There were so many to choose from, but she settled on a couple that would give her more information on the Lakota and on the Wounded Knee Massacre. Thanks to Chase, she'd become very interested in the Natives' struggle over the past couple of centuries and wished to learn more. A part of her also realized it was a way to keep a part of Chase with her when she was back home, never to see him again.

Before long, the afternoon had disappeared and they were on their way back to her hotel.

"I need to get ready for the event tonight. Will you be able to get to the fairgrounds on your own?"

"I can take the trolley like I did last night."

"That's perfect. I'll have Brandon keep an eye out for you and then I'll drive you back after."

"Sounds like a plan, but I can take the trolley back if you'd rather."

He cast a sidelong glance at her, a frown giving him lines between his brows. "Why would I rather? Didn't you have a good day with me?"

She quickly reassured him. "Oh, yes. I did. Very much. I just. Well, I didn't want you to feel obligated or anything."

He focused on the road ahead, grinding his jaw slightly before he spoke. "I don't do anything I don't want to do. I don't get where this is coming from. Especially when you said you enjoyed the day with me."

Aurora sighed. *Just say it.* Taking another breath, she forced herself to state the doubts that clung to her throughout the day. "You don't do anything you don't want to?"

"That's right!" He almost growled at her as he affirmed his previous statement.

"So, then, you didn't want to be with me last night." It wasn't a question, but an affirmation of her belief.

"What?" He turned to look at her, then dawning slid over his features. "Oh. You mean the kiss."

She nodded silently, her heart speeding up with nervousness.

Now he sighed. "Let's just say that I wanted to but there were other things to consider. I didn't want to take advantage of you. I know you were willing, I had other things, and it wouldn't have been fair to you," he repeated.

"What things?"

"I can't tell you. I'm sorry. But, it's not you. I swear."

She pressed her lips together and turned to look out the window. Whenever some guy says it's not her, it always was.

They drove silently for a bit, then he pulled over. "Look, bison."

True, she was upset and even being a bit childish, pouting slightly. She couldn't help it. It was just one more rejection in her life, and his aloofness did nothing to alleviate her own doubts of self-worth. She didn't understand and he didn't seem to care that he'd hurt her, even if that wasn't his intent.

But, seeing the large magnificent animals did brighten her back up. Her camera already in hand, she lifted it, snapping pictures of the huge beasts. After several dozen photos were taken, Chase grabbed her hand and her attention away from the animals.

"Look. I'm sorry if I hurt you last night. I'm sure from my original response you knew I wanted you. At least I thought you did. It's not that I don't want you. I really like spending time with you, being with you. Too much, maybe."

"Too much?"

"I've got obligations."

"You're married? Engaged then?"

He laughed. "Good god, no. I'm not a creep. Let's just say they're cultural responsibilities and leave it at that. Okay? Let me drive you to your hotel after the finals? Please?"

"Okay." She took a breath and squeezed his hand. "I'd like that." She knew he'd be leaving tomorrow morning, and she really wanted every minute with him she could get. Plus, she realized the cultural issues were probably because she wasn't Lakota or any other kind of Native American. The Lakota seemed a very proud people, albeit, Chase was the only Native she knew. Still, as such, he'd take their ideals to heart, and being with one who wasn't Native probably went against everything he stood for. She needed to let her anxiousness go and enjoy what he gave her for the short time they still had.

He brought her hand up to his lips, kissing her knuckles, then kept her hand in his to lie upon his lap as he pulled out and started driving again.

"I'm glad we got to see some bison. They're so big."

"Do you like them?"

"I'd never seen one before. I love all different kinds of animals. It's why I started in photography. I wanted to capture their essence for eternity."

He gave her a lopsided grin and squeezed her hand. "I'm very glad to hear you say that. Animals are very important to me as well."

"I hate how people take them for granted or, worse, abuse them. It infuriates me. Animals and babies. Both are dependent on us to love and care for them, not use or abuse them."

"Yep. I feel the same way. They gift us with sustenance, but they should be respected in every way. Hey, look, there are some more."

Aurora squealed excitedly. Chase was about to pull over again, but Aurora prevented him. "I know you need to get ready for the event."

"Thank you," he acknowledged and continued back to her hotel without any further diversions.

At least until they reached the Franklin Hotel. Outside the building was an ambulance and a group of onlookers.

"I wonder what's happened," Aurora whispered almost to herself.

"Have your room key out so they know you're staying here and not some nosy photographer trying to be some ambulance chaser."

Aurora smirked at the twinkle in his eye at his

apparent nuances. "I hadn't thought of it, but I certainly don't want to get in their way or be detained myself."

She grabbed her camera bag and jumped out of the truck. "I'll see you later."

He nodded as she shut the door before he drove off. Concerned she would be getting in the way, she carefully made her way up the porch, showing her key in order to bypass several already crowding the landing. Once inside, it wasn't as congested and she was grateful the throngs of people were mostly kept outside, even though the main floor had an active casino.

She had to show her room key again when she was ready to get on the elevator.

"What floor are you going to?" one of the policemen asked her.

"Third."

His eyes narrowed. "What room?"

His suspicion made her believe whatever was going on was on the floor she currently occupied. "Room 333."

"I better escort you to your room," he stated, climbing into the elevator car with her.

Aurora was quiet for a moment, then turned to the officer as the elevator made its slow, creaking assent. He was a middle-aged man with a rotund belly and a big mustache. "Is everything okay?" She knew it was a stupid question to ask. There obviously wouldn't be as many police and medical staff around if everything was just fine and dandy. "I mean. I hope whatever has happened, the person will be okay."

"Sorry, ma'am. Can't really talk about it. However, I would like to get your name, just in case our detectives would like to talk to you later."

The doors slid open and Aurora stepped out. "Me? Why would they want to speak with me?"

"You never know. This is the start of an investigation and they will probably be asking several people if they might have seen or heard anything. Your name?"

"Oh. Of course." She was a bit surprised, but hoisting her camera bag higher onto her shoulder, she turned to him. "Aurora Taylor. I doubt if I'll be much help. I've been gone all day."

"Where will you be this evening?"

"I'm attending the PBR event. Then maybe dinner or something."

"Is there a phone number for you?"

"Sure. My cell is 314-555-2618." She could see one of the rooms opened down the hallway and a crowd of officers, both in uniforms as well as plain clothes with their badges clipped to their belts in visible sight, milling about. She frowned. That room was awfully close to where she was staying; far closer than she was really comfortable with, especially since she didn't know what might've occurred just steps from her own door.

"Thank you." The officer turned and headed towards the group, handing off her information.

She rushed to her own room, quickly slipping inside. Her curiosity was certainly piqued, but a part of her didn't want to know either. Her woman's intuition told her whatever happened was dreadful and she was best not knowing.

Glancing at the clock, she realized she didn't have much time to think about it without being late to the rodeo.

Chapter Four

Aurora stepped off the trolley, but she barely took a couple of steps towards the entrance to the PBR stadium when a man approached her. Warily, she looked him over as he strode so purposefully in her direction, slightly concerned about his intent.

"Ms. Taylor?" He pulled his tan cowboy hat off, gripping it tightly between weathered hands. His dark brown hair was dusty despite being under his hat, making her wonder what he was doing to get so much dirt in his locks.

Then she remembered Chase was going to have one of his friends meet her and take her to the family and friends section of the arena. She smiled. "Brandon?"

He grinned back, his teeth glistening in the fading sunlight. "Ma'am. I'm to escort you to the VIP viewing area. This way." He put his hat back on and swept his arm out to indicate the direction of the private gated area.

She realized he was giving her several sidelong glances as they walked. Slightly exasperated, she turned to him as they walked. "I promise I won't try and climb in the pen with the bulls today. I don't plan on being mischievous in any way."

He laughed, a deep resonant sound not unpleasant to her ears. "Sorry, ma'am. I wasn't worried about you shacking up with the bulls. I apologize if I was unseemly. Just, well, ain't never been one of Chase's gals or anyone for him here 'fore."

"You must know him pretty well then."

"A tad, I reckon. We grew up together." He chuckled his response.

She couldn't help but chuckle with him. "Just a tad then, I guess. So, do I meet with your approval then?" She gave him a glance before she turned to climb the steps up to the seating area.

He gave her a longer, piercing look, tilting his head slightly. His eyes were dark and his features hard to read, but somehow, she didn't think he approved of her at all despite his apparent kindness. "Ain't mine to give," he stated blandly, then pointed to the gated area. "Ya can enjoy the event from here. If ya need anything to eat or drink, just ask one of the hands at the rail."

He'd seemed pleasant enough when he greeted her at the trolley, but now his manner was cold and she wondered if she offended him somehow. "Thank you. I'm sure I'll be fine."

He tapped his hat with his forefinger and headed down to the arena. Perplexed, she found a seat and looked around, searching for Chase or even Brandon. She couldn't overcome the feeling Brandon's disapproval, for whatever reason, would be a bone of contention between the men, and she had no desire to be a nuisance to Chase in any way during the last few hours she'd have with him.

Brandon was soon out of sight, and she realized he'd gone to the changing area that was hidden behind the chutes, where the riders prepared for their turn.

"Don't mind him. He gets focused on his job and forgets how to be a pleasant human."

Aurora turned around to peer at the young man sitting behind her with a box of popcorn, munching away. He appeared to be in his late teens or early twenties at best. A bit of scruff on his chin with piercing dark brown eyes, she wondered who he might be here for, since he was in the family section.

"You know him then? Brandon?"

He guffawed, tossing a piece of popcorn into the air to catch it with his mouth. "Guess you could say that. He's my brother."

Aurora felt the heat seep into her cheeks. "Oh." She knew she hadn't said anything untoward against him, but she had *thought* it.

The man laughed harder. "Don't worry about it. He makes most people feel inferior. I'm Kyle." He rubbed his salted hand across his plaid-shirted chest and held it out to her.

"Aurora." She took his slightly buttery, proffered hand, giving it a light shake.

"Oh. You're the one who almost became meat on a stick by Devil yesterday." It was a statement more than a question. Kyle knew everything that happened since Chase and Aurora met yesterday.

Admittedly, Kyle was curious about why Chase was so enthralled with her and why the elders were so concerned over this mere human. She was admittedly cute. A bit too pudgy for his personal tastes, but then, he wasn't interested in her for that reason.

"True. I assume it's why I seem to have so many eyes watching me since I arrived."

Kyle's lips curled. Standing, he hopped the row of chairs and plopped down next to her. He wasn't about to admit it was Chase's tribal band and not the antics with the bulls that caused her to be watched so closely. She didn't need to know that, nor did she need to know why Kyle volunteered for this job. "It is. Chase will be one of the last in order to keep his place, so you might as well get comfy."

She sighed and turned her attention back to the arena and the bullfighters that were being introduced. The riders then came out, Chase among them. He nodded ever so slightly in her direction, then turned to face the flag, hat in hand, as the national anthem was sung. The riders headed back behind the chutes and gates to await their turn. Brandon and the other bullfighters remained along the fence line to swiftly jump in when a rider was thrown from or jumped off the bull.

She had to give Brandon credit for the work he did in getting the bulls away from the rider so quickly. She gasped in horror as one bull actually flipped a rider with his head when he'd fallen off. The rider got up relatively quickly, despite the injury he must've sustained, the announcer declaring the rider was only stunned, but fine.

The incident made her worry about Chase. She honestly didn't know how she'd handle it if she had to watch him get hurt in such a way. The sport was so dangerous, and although thrilling, it was also disconcerting. She noticed Chase standing on the guard rails and fence alternatively during the rides, and occasionally she'd catch his eye, but he'd quickly look away, somewhat guiltily, she thought. She wondered if Brandon had said something to him about her, or if she was just being a bit paranoid.

Chase was almost the last to ride, and by the time it was his turn, she was antsy in her concern for him. This was really the first time she'd sat through this type of event. The first time she had the opportunity to see it was last night and most of that was spent in the back area with the guards and others. Was that really just last night? It seemed a lifetime ago and yet, time seemed fleeting as well, for soon enough he'd be gone from her life.

When Chase climb into the chute and onto the bull, he didn't even look her way. His head was down, his hat low on his head. She assumed he was focusing on what he needed to do. He had a good chance at first place, according to the announcer, and this ride would determine his standing.

Brandon was on the edge of the field, ready to jump in to distract the bull once Chase was off his back. She found it ironic that Chase was riding Devil, the very bull that charged her the previous evening.

"Chase is on one of the meanest bulls around. Devil certainly lives up to his name, but if Chase can hold him for his eight, he could move into first place, depending on his final score. Or Devil could kill him," the announcer stated matter of factly.

Aurora knew he was just trying to drum up the suspense, but she was already on the edge of her seat; she didn't need him to make it worse. She couldn't help but notice the look Brandon and Chase seemed to exchange and that only made her more anxious.

Kyle must've sensed her nervousness as he leaned over to pat her arm. "Don't worry. He's a professional."

She knew he was trying to be comforting, but for some reason it only made her more anxious.

Chase's eight seconds seemed to last an eternity. She was sure it didn't help that she held her breath the moment the gate opened and the bull roared out, bucking furiously. It was only when Chase was safely behind the fence did she release the air she'd unconsciously stopped.

Kyle leaned over when the scores came up. "Chase came in second place. The last two riders can, at best, maybe get third place if they score high enough, but Chase is secure in his standing."

She had arranged to meet him after he rode. So after the last rider had finished and the winners announced, Aurora headed to their predetermined location, followed closely by Kyle, her self-appointed body guard.

"Get off my back, Brandon."

She stopped when she heard Chase's snarl, staying out of their line of sight.

"You know better, dude. Why are you putting yourself through this? You know the deal."

"Do you really think I don't know? The elders already paid me a visit to remind me too. I know damn well what I can and can't have, but I'll be damned if I don't take what I can get."

"I don't get it, bro. What is she doing to you?"

"Bran, I wish I knew. I don't understand it myself, but I can't say goodbye. Not yet. I know I have to, but not yet."

The two men glared at each other silently for a few long moments, then Brandon sighed. "Just be careful, bro. All I'm saying is I don't want to see you hurt again. Not like before."

"I won't. I don't plan on letting it get anywhere near that far." Chase pulled off his hat and ran a hand through his hair. "I'm not ready to let her go just yet. I don't know why. There's something about her that *he* needs."

Brandon was quiet, then his eyes slid past Chase to meet Aurora's. Chase seemed to sense she was there as well as he turned to meet her curious, concerned gaze, noticing Kyle behind her as well. A moment of jealousy flooded Chase's body. He didn't want another man, especially a younger one like Kyle, to be anywhere near her. "What's he doing with her?"

"Keeping an eye on her since I was focused on the bulls not killing any of you," Brandon spat. He moved past Chase towards Aurora. When he reached Kyle and her, he appeared to snarl at her, grabbing Kyle's arm. "Let's go."

She didn't approach Chase, unsure of whether or not he wanted her to.

Chase sighed and moved closer to her. "You overheard."

It was a statement, not a question, but she nodded affirmatively.

"I'm sorry you had to hear that."

"I'm sorry if I'm causing problems."

"You're not. We've been like brothers for so long, he likes to mother me sometimes. Look, don't worry about it. I'd like to go and wash up and then we can go out to dinner. Okay? Just as we planned. Please." He pleaded as if his life depended on it.

She gave him a small smile. "Of course." She took his proffered arm and walked by his side as they headed towards his truck, wondering who 'he' was and what 'he' needed that Chase wanted her nearby for 'him.' She also wondered if that was part of the cultural obligation Chase informed her of earlier. Maybe Chase was getting her ready for 'him?' Somehow, that made her extremely uncomfortable for a brief moment.

But then, Chase fought to be with her, against Brandon and maybe even Kyle. The whole thing was confusing and it hurt her head to try and figure it out. Instead, she decided to take a deep breath and focus and what she wanted: to enjoy the last few hours she had with Chase.

Comfortable by his side, she couldn't help feeling Brandon's eyes on her back.

Chapter Five

Aurora's hands slid up his back as their kiss deepened. She couldn't help be surprised and extremely disappointed when he pushed her back as he had the previous evening, breaking their contact. She looked at him questioningly, unsure and a bit disheartened. At least this time he'd escorted her to her room first. He'd stated he was concerned over her due to the incident at the hotel earlier, albeit, neither knew what it fully entailed other than a woman was found dead by the hotel staff.

Chase took a moment to get himself under control. He could feel her concern and her uncertainty. "I'm sorry. I just don't want to start something I can't finish."

Her features changed immediately to sympathetic understanding. "Oh. I'm sorry. I didn't know. Didn't understand. It's nothing to be ashamed about. And doctors can help now-a-days."

Chase peered at her bewildered. "Doctors?" Then realization dawned on him of what she thought. "God damn it, woman. You think I'm impotent? I'm not. I can perform just fine, thank you very much." He was highly insulted. If she only knew the truth, he'd screw her so hard she wouldn't be able to walk for several days.

He was angry at her assumption, but what was Aurora to think? "Oh." She lowered her eyes and started to move away from him. It wasn't that he couldn't get it up; it was that he didn't want to for her.

Chase grabbed her arm before she got too far from him. "I should explain. I've had one-night stands with many women. But, Aurora, I don't want that with you. I don't want to wham, bam, thank you, ma'am to you, but I can't give you anything more than that." He pulled his hat off and ran a hand through his luscious hair. "I'm probably not explaining this very well. I apologize for my inadequacy."

Aurora shook her head. "No, I get it." She didn't believe him. "I wasn't asking for anything more from you other than a night or two and I assumed you were probably leaving tomorrow since the finals were completed tonight. I wasn't going to chase you down and ask for more. You've got your life. I've got mine. I got it." Aurora turned away again. Hurt and humiliated.

Faster than she thought humanly possible, he was in front of her blocking her path, his hands on her biceps.

"I don't think you do. I can tell you're hurt and upset and that's not what I wanted. I didn't want to start something more with you because I wanted more *from* you. I didn't want to have to remember what I have to give up when I leave, and being intimate with you is only going to make walking away from you that much harder. I'm not strong enough. Not for that. Not for you. I know we just met yesterday, but over the last thirty hours I've grown to know you better, and I find you hard to resist. Just don't ask me to explain why."

Aurora was confused once again. The sincerity in his voice, the strong intensity of his words, and the desire for her to understand made her question everything. Was it because he was Indian and she wasn't? Was it their cultural differences that kept him from being with her? Maybe it was their living locations of several states apart? "I wasn't asking for or expecting anything beyond a couple of hours of being with you," she repeated softly.

"I know. And normally, it wouldn't even be a question or issue. But you're different. I don't want to say goodbye so quickly, and I'll have to leave soon enough as it is." He dropped his hands from her. "Please. Aurora, please don't go. Don't walk away from me. Not yet."

Aurora couldn't remember the last time she was so unsure of herself or her own feelings. She'd had men refuse her before and she'd had men happy with a one-night stand. Mostly because that's all they wanted from her anyway. Chase was so opposite of the men she'd met previously, and yet at this moment there was a weakness to him that tugged at her heart. She couldn't deny him, no matter how much she wanted to. "Sure," she finally managed to get out.

They stood facing each other for a moment that

seemed more like an eternity to her. Her own doubt of her self-worth still lingered in the air and she felt disheartened. She should probably say something, anything to break the heavy silence that wrapped around them like a thick fog. His last few words gave her pause, but her hope had been shattered too often in the past. She didn't trust him to not mean what he said. She knew there were prettier, thinner girls he could have his pick from, so why he chose to be with her confounded her.

"Fuck it," he growled, and collided into her body, pushing her farther into her room and kicking the door shut while propelling her back against the wall as his lips devoured hers with a desperate need, a thirst only she was going to quell.

Aurora had no clue what changed or happened. One moment she was feeling unsure and confused and the next he had her pressed up against the wall, kissing her as if he were a man just let out of prison after being alone for centuries.

Chase gripped her wrists and pulled them over her head. His knee pushed her thighs apart. He kissed her so hard, so furiously, she was lost to him. His mouth moved along her jaw to her ear.

"Tell me to stop. Tell me no," he whispered, begging for any reason to not go further. The warning he was given by the elders earlier in the day and the argument he had with Brandon mere hours ago did nothing to alleviate the ache of his desire.

She lifted her head exposing her neck to him. "Yes. Please. Oh, God, yes."

Any restraint he had was gone the moment she spoke those five little words. He hoped she wouldn't be too angry with him, but he was beyond caring. The beast inside roared to life, his hooves pounding the earth within his body. He released her hands and gripped her shirt, tearing it in two, tossing the pieces to the floor. He repeated the process with her bra, freeing her rosy globes. His hand captured one while his mouth the other and almost groaned at the taste of her. He played with her nipple, feeling it harden under his tongue.

Aurora slipped her hands in his hair, sliding his

hat off his head and onto the floor along with her tattered clothing.

He let his lips glide across her chest from one breast to the other, her nipple already tender and hard from his teasing hand. He flicked and sucked at her breasts with a fierceness his inner beast demanded of him.

She'd questioned his desire for her, his ability to appease her, his aptitude to perform. He'd prove her wrong over and over again, until she begged him to stop. As a spirit walker, he didn't take long to recharge and could give her multiple orgasms, as well as take them for himself.

He straightened up and grabbed her hand to place it on his bulging crotch. "Have no doubt. This is what you do to me. It's too late to turn back now. Tonight, you're mine."

He took a step back after releasing her hand, pivoted slightly and scooped her up, carrying her to the bed. He heard her gasp when he picked her up so easily. She'd no idea of who or what he was, and she couldn't ever know the full truth, but he had to have her now. If only for tonight, he just had to. He went against the elders all his life, forging a new path for himself. What was one final act of defiance?

He was done being gentle, finished playing by the rules when it came to Aurora. Somehow, she'd crawled her way into his very soul and he had to have all of her, even if it was just for one glorious night of unbelievable pleasure that would have to last him an eternity. For him, that was longer than the human mind could even process. But he didn't care, his need outweighed any consequences there might be. Even if the pain was only in his heart and soul from having to release her.

He set her on the bed, leaning over to pull her jeans and panties off, leaving her exposed to his devouring eyes. He committed her to memory, for this was all he'd have for many years to come. He was out of his clothes and on top of her in an instant. Now. Now was the time to go slower, or so he planned, but his animal had other ideas. He rubbed his hands over her smooth skin. Feeling her writhe under him put him in overdrive. The soft moans and cries she made as he touched her made him lose himself. He wanted her. He wanted to taste her and prepare her human opening for his large member.

Licking and suckling, he made his way down the length of her body, settling himself before her red, needy apex. Her aroused scent sent him into blessed madness. He licked around her nether lips, tasting her seeping juices. Thrusting a finger deep into her recesses, he fucked her with his digit. He added a second, third, and then a fourth, stretching her out to accommodate his cock when he felt she was ready.

She arched and cried out, gripping the sheets and his head as she writhed, convulsing under his ministrations, but he didn't stop or slow down. Instead, he opened her wider with his hand. She stiffened and yelped, but he was beyond caring. He pushed in and felt her relax, then move with him, meeting his thrusting hand with each movement.

Almost. She was almost ready for him. "Come

on, baby. Let it go again," he encouraged her, and she listened, stiffening momentarily before her body's juices came crashing like waves against his hand buried deep inside her core. He could feel her muscles contract as she arched against him.

"I hope you're not done yet. I've only just begun," he growled between sucking her juices off each individual digit.

"I'm ready and waiting," she responded, albeit a bit hoarsely.

He cocked a smile. She might think she was ready, but she had no idea what he was going to do to her tonight. He positioned himself above her, spreading her legs a bit wider to accommodate his larger frame, and plunged into her heated depths, his cock hitting the walls of her very womb.

She wriggled under him, squirmed and arched against his rapid pistoning movements. A slight sheen of sweat covered her body, giving her a salty taste as he continued to let his tongue glide against her neck and shoulder.

Her hands gripped his ass as if encouraging

him further. He didn't need the incentive, but he went faster, his movements almost entering the preternatural realm of speed. He slipped in and out so rapidly he knew she was going to be sore, but he'd deal with it later. For now, he was too close. He just needed her to come for him again. His mouth and hands licked, pinched, and squeezed, almost abusing her body with untold pleasures. Her guttural responses only inspired him to continue. Since it was her third orgasm, it took her a bit longer to achieve it, but that was totally fine with him.

He gripped her hands and stretched them over her head, elongating her body under him. He was close. So very close, feeling the blood rush and swell his cock even more. He nipped at her shoulder, giving a touch of pain to her pleasure. He could feel her freeze before she screamed out her release. Her juices washed over him and heated his ready prick as he grunted his own release.

Although he pumped his seed into her, he knew he was still engorged inside of her. She panted and he loosened his grip, holding still over her. Cocking a smile, he let his finger lightly trace her lips. "We're not done."

Her eyes widened. He was kidding, right? She knew he came, his sticky seed was mingling with her own juices as they dripped onto her thighs and into the sheets beneath her. However, she wasn't going to deny him or herself of such an unbelievable lover. "Bring it."

He chuckled at her bravado. He rolled over, taking her with him until she was settled on top with him still swollen inside her.

She was about to slip off him in order to slide down his body and place her mouth over his manhood, but he wasn't about to have any of it. He held her hips down on him and used his strength to lift her slightly before pushing her back down again. She didn't waste time; understanding exactly what he wanted of her, she quickly took the lead. She continued to move on him, riding him like the beast he was.

He held onto her thighs and leaned back,

shutting his eyes, enjoying the feeling she was stirring within him. His animal pranced about inside; his intent on claiming this woman had finally manifested and the animal within wasn't about to let her go until she was so sore she'd feel it for days and think of him with every movement of her aching body.

Chase had always held back, not wanting to hurt the mortal women he'd lain with. His first time with a mortal, he didn't know or understand how much more fragile they were compared to those who were blessed by the Great Mystery. He'd plunged in with all the desperation she seemed to have but he hadn't prepped her for his size and wounded her opening, causing intense pain followed by death as she bled out days later.

He thought it was her, so tried again a couple of years later. This time taking the time needed to open her up to his cock before he plunged in. At first, things were fine, but his desperation caused a speed that rubbed her so raw she had internal bleeding and became feverish, succumbing to the illness within days.

Chase remained celibate for decades after that. Although he'd been with women of his own ilk, they weren't his mate calling to his soul. And once he came on the circuit, he had many women chasing after him for his favors. He'd learned to be more cautious with human women, but he also learned to only go so far so as not to permanently, mortally damage them.

Chase may be a spirit walker, but he was also a man with needs and desires as any other. The next few human women he laid with, he was careful to prep first, just as he had Aurora. But none had lasted beyond four or five orgasms, not the way he did them. Riding him would pretty much be the end of his time with her.

Although excited when she came the fourth time, his inner bison also knew from previous experience he might only be able to get one or two more shots off. Then Chase would have to corral his beast yet again. He knew this time his animal wouldn't go so docilely. He should be concerned about the growing attachment, but Aurora felt too good on him to worry about it now. He just wanted her to build so he could push her at least one more time into the heavens of ecstasy.

He could feel every movement she made as she encased his thickness. He let her go at her own pace until he could stand it no more. He needed her to come again and he needed to give in to his own desire. He pushed himself up, forcing her back onto the bed. Then, remaining inside her, he placed his legs outside of her own, twisting her on his cock so she was now face down on the mattress. Lifting her waist up so she could get on all fours, he drove into her while rubbing her swollen clit from the underside. With his other arm, he held her around her waist, feeling her weaken and tire slightly and needing her somewhat stable as he drove repeatedly into her.

"Will you come for me again?" he asked softly against her ear from behind, quickly giving her sex a hard slap to let the sting of pain mingle with the pleasure of everything else.

She squealed as the ache throbbed through her core, letting her eyes go back into her head for a split moment as the sensation raced along her nerve endings. "Faster," she managed to get out. "Again."

He knew what she meant by faster and readily obliged her by picking up speed. Again took him a moment to register. She wanted to be slapped again, enjoying the mingling of pleasure and pain. He acquiesced, slapping her again on her sex, then a bit harder on her ass. She groaned with each punishment and soon gripped the sheets as she bucked against him. She didn't scream out like she did the last time, but she did moan, and somehow that thrilled him more than her screams. She froze, then jerked in his arms as she came. Her warming liquid was just the heat he needed to finish up as well. He continued to pump every vestige of seed he had to give, then forced himself to think of things other than the fantastic woman he still held. He helped her lay face down in bed, then slowly pulled out, releasing another gasp from her with the popping sound of being free from his heated thickness.

The cold air hit his cock immediately, but he didn't care. His blood still ran hot in his desire for more of her. Softly, he brushed the hair off her face as he kissed her cheek. "Let me clean you up. Don't move."

Aurora mumbled her acknowledgement. She watched him go to the bathroom, get a washcloth, wet it and bring it and a towel back. She was exhausted. How he had the energy to move about so easily was a conundrum to her. Every part of her ached, tingled, shivered and missed him. She couldn't help but notice his manhood was still pretty erect, glistening from both of them. She wasn't a virgin, but she'd never seen a man erect for so long or so quickly after achieving his own release. She may be a lot of things, but there was no way in hell she wasn't going to help him deflate and be satisfied. Somehow. Someway. She wiped her eyes and sat up as he returned.

He gently spread her legs apart and used the wet cloth to wipe her. He sniffed the air and checked the cloth and bedding around her to make sure he hadn't caused her to bleed. "Probably should've used a condom. Sorry about that."

"Truthfully, I was too surprised and caught up in the moment to even think of it. Don't worry though. I do take birth control. I'm clean too." She could only pray he was also free from any sexually transmitted diseases, considering his admission of several one-night stands.

He arched his brow and cocked that smile she'd grown to adore. "I'm clean too." In truth, spirit walkers didn't get human diseases. It was one of their many gifts from the Great Mystery, as well as longevity and being able to shift into their spirit guides, attaining all the attributes of their animal. And, although birth control didn't work on his kind, he didn't think it possible he got her pregnant.

He dropped the cloth on the floor and reached for the towel he'd brought with him. She blocked him by leaning over and gripping the wet cloth from the floor. Standing, she pivoted around, shoving him onto the bed in a sitting position.

"I never said I was done."

He gave her a shocked look as she used the cloth to wipe down his hard manhood. He didn't know what to say, so he said nothing. At this point, he'd let her guide any additional activity she had in mind, not wanting to hurt her in any way and yet amazed she still wanted to be intimate with him. Astounded she even had the energy.

His cock sprang further to life upon hearing her words, twitching in anticipation, becoming fuller and even a bit longer. She looked at it, impressed at his veracity. She moved between his legs and knelt down. He frowned and reached out to pull her up. "You don't have to. I'll be okay."

She tilted her head. She'd never heard of a man who didn't like getting sucked. Was it a cultural taboo or something more personal? Either way, she would oblige him. "I'm not done," she repeated. "But I'll abide your wishes of not sucking you off."

Instead, she moved to kneel over him, her heat tickling his own erection. He stood, gripping her by the ass and taking her with him. She wrapped her legs around his waist, surprised at being lifted this way. She wasn't a small woman, yet he maneuvered her about as if she was a mere child. He positioned his cock against her opening, tantalizing her with his hardness. Then he impaled her on him as he walked to the table near the window. It was three in the morning. If anyone were watching them screw at this time of night, they could enjoy the show as far as he was concerned. Once she was seated on the small piece of furniture, he began to repeatedly plunge into her. Her legs held him against her. He still couldn't believe that she was still able and willing to take more of him.

The table shook under them both and he hoped it would hold up to the abuse they were giving it. It was never made for something like this, he was sure, but somehow he knew he wasn't the first to use it for something other than its original purpose.

Before long, they both came almost at the same time. But she could still feel how engorged he was and she knew something wasn't right. Again he pulled out of her, but kissed her without moving away.

"Chase? Can I ask you something personal?"

He paused, then sighed and looked up at her. "I might not answer, but you can always ask." He had a good idea what she wanted to know.

She chuckled. "Not answering is always a possibility, but I have to try. I was wondering if you've taken something. I mean, it's really not natural to still be this ready after coming three times, and I know you have, because I feel your seed in me when you get off."

"No. I didn't take anything. I don't need to. I'm just a unique male who has a very thin window of down time."

"How many times? How long?"

He shrugged. "I don't know. I usually only go two, three or four, depending on the woman I am with. Most just roll over and so they never realized I could still keep going. Let me think of a couple of non-erotic things, like my mother, and it'll go down. You don't have to worry about it."

She tilted her head. "Two, three or four, huh?

But you don't know? And this is natural?"

"Well, um, yeah. It's not induced by anything artificial. I swear to that."

"Hmm. You know, I've always been one for the strange and unique, and I've always been up for a challenge. Should we see how many you can have before you finally calm down on your own without thinking non-erotic thoughts?"

His eyes widened in surprise and his beast inside stood at attention. "That's not necessary," he finally said after he took a moment to calm his being down.

"Good. Challenge accepted. Now let me think, that was three for you and five for me. Hmm. You're two behind, but since you won't let me suck you off, I guess I'll just remain in the lead for two. In the meantime, let's see how many more we can have together." She spread her legs wider, planting her heels on the edge of the table and exposing her dripping sex to his hungry eyes.

He swallowed hard. "You don't know what you're asking. I could hurt you."

"I do know. I admit, you're a big man, but all this activity has stretched me out pretty good and I've got the stamina. I don't think you can hurt me at this point. I might not be able to walk for a couple of days, but who the hell cares? Are you going to take me up on the challenge, or always wonder what your final number orgasm will be?"

He didn't move, watching her closely. Was she kidding? Or being genuinely serious? Either way, he couldn't. He couldn't take the chance no matter how enticing the idea was to him. He wasn't sure she realized the consequences of what she was asking, but then she reached down and started rubbing herself and he almost dropped to his knees in supplication. He'd have to keep a bit of himself reined in, making sure he didn't hurt her by accident. He knew he couldn't live with himself if something happened to her. He growled and pushed her hand away, putting his own where hers had just been and slipping a couple of fingers inside.

He played with her for a moment, then scooped her off the table and let her bend down, overlooking

Main Street below. He entered her from behind, using his hands to hide her sex while he rubbed it, his arm across her ample breasts.

By the time the sun had risen and her nine am alarm sounded off, they had copulated for hours and he had come twelve more times. He'd never thought it possible to find someone, especially a human woman, who could keep up with him every step of the way. He was flabbergasted and couldn't be happier if he were in his right mind.

He actually felt himself waning and knew sixteen would be the end of it. At least for him. Aurora might be able to continue, although how, he still had no clue. She was surprising and amazing. He hated having to give her up after this night, but fuck if this night wouldn't last him for a multitude of decades.

He had her pressed against the cold tile of the shower. He was near and so was she. This time, they might actually come together. He somehow knew they were both that close. He gripped her hair and pulled her head back exposing her neck. He wanted to bite her neck, suckle her blood and make her his for all time. He thought about giving her a hickey instead, but he didn't think she'd appreciate being branded by him, even if only temporarily. He had no right to claim her. He had only promised her tonight, a night he should never have had with her. Was this what the elders feared? His growing attachment? His thoughts of leaving the band for her? Or even claiming her, a human into a special band of Lakota? He forced those thoughts out of his head. He only needed to concentrate on her and make her feel as phenomenal as she did him.

"I'm going to come," he growled fiercely, pulling on her hair even harder.

She gripped his hair as well, pulling it with a ferocity he didn't think she had. Her moans deepened and she gripped him tighter with her legs. She came, her voice hoarse from all the crying out she'd been doing over the past several hours. Then she seemed to slump against him. He pushed into her a final time, feeling his seed eject into her deeply red and burning core. Then something happened to him as well. He seemed to leave his body and float above both of them, only she was there floating as well.

Never had he had an orgasm so strong he left his own body. Never had he experienced anything like the bliss he was now feeling, his essence intertwining with hers. Was it a dream? A result of pure exhaustion? Pure ecstasy? His imagination? Whatever it was, it was over just as quickly as it had appeared and he was back in the shower holding her against the cool tiles. Slowly he pulled out and his cock, for the first time since they got to her hotel room last night, was finally deflated.

She looked down at him. "Guess sixteen is the magic number."

Chapter Six

She reached her hand out and the emptiness of the space beside her startled her enough to open her eyes. The bed was empty. Chase was nowhere in the room. For a brief moment, she wondered if the whole thing was a dream. That was, until she tried to move in order to see what time it was. Every muscle in her frame cried out in agony. Yep, he was with her and worked her so hard she knew her body wasn't going to let her forget him any time soon, as if she could ever forget him.

My god, that man was virile. She'd thought what they did throughout the night into the morning hours was impossible. Aurora figured she'd be lucky to find a man who could keep up with her, but she was amazed she could keep up with him. Not that it was an issue. She knew she'd never see him again, and though her loins were disappointed, as was her heart, the former also needed time to recoup. Alright, probably days.

She struggled out of bed amidst a ton of moaning on her part and headed to the bathroom.

Another hot shower and some Advil should calm down the aches enough to feel somewhat normal and get her work done.

Stuck to her mirror was a note with her name on it in a strong but very clear distinct masculine cursive. Smiling, she grabbed it. Maybe the note would tell her he'd be back to see her before she left in two days. Excitedly, she opened the folded piece of paper to read as she sat on the toilet.

Aurora,

No words can ever describe what last night meant to me. You're as beautiful on the inside as you are out and I wish my circumstances allowed me more time to be with you.

Yet, part of me is glad we can't be together more, because leaving you now is unbelievably difficult. A few more days with you, even one, would be nigh on impossible.

I wish I were a stronger man to defy my customs or even my people, but

I'm not.

Words alone could never apologize enough. I'm sorry I snuck out without saying goodbye or telling you in person how special last night was, but again with you, my beautiful Aurora, I'm not a strong man.

I hope one day you'll understand and look favorably upon this memory.

Chase

Aurora read the letter three more times before placing it on the bathroom sink. She was going to crumple it and throw it away, but she realized she wanted to remember this for all her life. And as silly as it sounded, this was a piece of him she could treasure for all eternity.

Popping some Advil and taking a hot shower, she got ready for her day on only a couple hours of sleep.

Her new travel mug was filled from the room's coffee pot and, checking on the water in the makeshift vase, she was ready to go to work.

In the elevator, she heard the other guests as they quietly whispered over the details of yesterday's incident.

"I heard the woman was strangled."

"How awful."

"Do you think we should worry?"

"Should we leave earlier than we planned?"

"Did they catch the guy?"

"Do they even know who did it?"

"Was she alone? Or travel here with someone?"

"Heard she was alone. From North Dakota, I think?"

"I heard she was here for the PBR and they think it might be someone who was also there."

"That's a lot of people to be looking at."

"I heard she was the second murder. There was another at the event grounds just a few nights ago."

"Really?"

"Probably all these people coming for the event that is bringing out the killers."

"Such a shame."

Once the elevator doors opened, Aurora

gratefully escaped, but she couldn't help wondering if the woman they were discussing was the same one she met a couple of nights ago. Could it be Allison? Met on the same night she died? She was from Bismarck. She was alone and visiting the PBR. Was it all a coincidence? Aurora hadn't realized Allison could've been just a couple of doors away from her room, but then again, she had the nagging feeling she did know. There was the vaguest déjà vu sense she saw Allison entering or departing that room, but for some reason Aurora couldn't really remember positively. How odd. Thinking about it further, she couldn't even remember getting to her own room and preparing for bed that night. She must've been too distracted with the broken kiss from Chase and the overall day's events, as well as the excitement of seeing Chase again the following day. What she did remember was having a bad night's sleep and actually sleepwalking. Did she see Allison in the hallway as a result? Why was everything feeling as if it was just teetering in the back of her mind? Did she see something that could help identify whoever committed such a horrific deed?

She headed the two blocks to her car, preferring to walk instead of using the complimentary golf cart. The sunshine and fresh air would assist in clearing her head from her cobwebbed thoughts. She was sure she was just being a bit paranoid since the woman was killed just doors from her own. It could've been Aurora murdered in her bed, or even in the hallway since she was walking around in a sleepy haze. She admonished herself over her morbid thoughts, needing to focus on something other than the murder at the Franklin.

Once at her vehicle, she set her GPS and drove towards the Wild Horse Sanctuary in Hot Springs, South Dakota. The drive was pleasant enough, but her mind couldn't stop thinking about Chase, and her body wouldn't let her. She was so focused on remembering him and their day together yesterday, she'd almost missed her turn off in Hot Springs.

As she neared the Sanctuary, she realized there appeared to be several Natives around. More so than she'd seen during her time at Crazy Horse. It only served to distract her more from her drive to thinking of Chase, and she knew she had a long, tough road ahead in forgetting him.

Thankfully, the signs for the Sanctuary were plentiful and she did her best to concentrate on her main reason she was in South Dakota to begin with.

Aurora always had a love for animals, and horses were her favorite since she was a child. To her, they epitomized strength, gentleness and beauty. They were majestic creatures who could be loyal and trusting to any soul kind to them.

A woman, graying at the temples, skin weathered by the sun, appeared on the porch of the main building as Aurora approached. Technically, they were closed on Sundays, which was why this was the best time to arrange to photograph the animals. Aurora had been foresighted enough to call ahead to remind the Sanctuary of her arrival, despite her original tardiness. She really needed at least a couple of hours of sleep before she was to meet with them. Regardless, as a result, she wasn't surprised to see someone was waiting for her.

Parking, she left her equipment in the vehicle as she went to greet the woman on the porch.

"Aurora?" the woman asked as she approached.

"Yes."

The woman smiled. "So glad to meet you. I'm Kelly. Come on in for a moment. I'll get my keys and we can start when you're ready."

"Perfect. If you don't mind, I'd be grateful if I could use the facilities first?"

"No problem. They're behind the building. Just watch out for the snakes."

"Snakes?"

"Yep. They're all around. If you stomp, they won't be surprised. They're more scared of you than you are of them."

"I highly doubt that." Aurora walked through the small one-room gift shop into the next room where the cash register was. Kelly gave Aurora some pamphlets and flyers on some of the different breeds that could be found at the Sanctuary before leading her out to the back and pointing where the truck would be waiting for her when she was finished.

Almost too scared at seeing a slithering snake to pee, she managed, then raced back to her car to get her equipment, only to meet Kelly at the truck.

The landscape was vast and beautiful.

"Let me give you a bit of basic background about us. A man by the name of Dayton O. Hyde saw the need to protect wild mustangs when he saw the conditions they were living in. In 1987, he'd gone to Nevada to buy some cattle and came across rounded-up mustangs, where they had been captured by the federal government and contained in a corral. He felt it was too cruel to take a wild horse away from their freedom and home just to be contained in a small, confined area. Mr. Hyde envisioned large tracts of land where the horses could be free once again. With the help of the South Dakota governor, he obtained this tract of land and established the Institute of Range and the American Mustang, also known as IRAM, in 1988. Today, we have eleven thousand acres for the horses to roam.

"We also take in abused and neglected breeds, but our focus is on the mustang. There are several varieties. The Spanish, which include the Barbary or Barb, the Sorraia, and the Andalusian. There are the American Mustangs, the Choctaw Ponies and the Curly Mustangs. Did you know the latter are also hypo-allergenic? Their hair was sometimes collected from the Curly to use for spinning yarn.

"The Choctaw Ponies are said to be the oldest. Their ancestry traces back to the Spanish horses that came over with the conquistadors in the sixteenth century. To the Choctaw people, this breed was symbolic of wealth, glory, honor and prestige. They are also the purest breeds, as the Choctaw were very careful about how the ponies were bred." Kelly pointed each of the breeds out as they passed them, giving Aurora the running commentary while Aurora kept snapping pictures, waving her hand when she needed Kelly to stop. Being the land of the horses, she was only allowed to take her pictures from the open window of the truck, but it didn't make her any less appreciative of the majestic beauty of the animals.

"I've noticed some markings on each of the horse's necks. Can you tell me about these?"

"Sure. The BLM or Bureau of Land Management, uses a freeze brand placed on the left side of the neck and is done with liquid nitrogen to tell the year of birth and the horse's registration. Each direction of the mark represents a different number. The two that are top and bottom are the birth year, and the symbols that are horizontal after the vertical ones are the registration number.

"Over there are some American Mustangs. The herd is led by the dominate mare as to where they graze, rest and travel to water. They are also the result of a lot of crossbreeding, which include draft horses, thoroughbreds, ranching horses, Indian ponies and Spanish types.

"Finally, the Spanish Mustangs can be traced back to the time of the Romans. Look over there. That's one of the few Sorraias here. There are only approximately two hundred left in the entire world, with less than one hundred reproducing mares. This is nowhere near what would ensure the survival of the most primitive Iberian horse we have today. They were named for the Sorraia River in Portugal where they were first seen in 1920 by a scientist and horse expert who discovered them, a Dr. Ruy d'Andrade."

Many of the horses watched them as they drove by while Kelly explained everything. At the top of one hill, Kelly paused. "If you want, you can get out for a couple of minutes here. That area you see on the other side of the Cheyenne River is where the wild horses are. These you've been looking at were donated or rescued for protection. We need the funds to help with their care, as well as acquire more."

"That's the whole idea behind this calendar. I'm taking so many pictures I should have several years of calendars for you to sell."

"I can't tell you how much we appreciate this. Every bit helps our cause."

"It's a worthy project and I'm happy to donate my time for such a great enterprise."

Aurora slipped one lens into her bag and grabbed her powerful double-power lens. Through the higher power, she could clearly see the wild and free horses across the valley, snapping away.

As she pivoted the camera to scan the area for more shots, she saw a glimmer of movement out of the corner of her eye. Turning the camera to focus on it, what she saw made her gasp and stand up straighter in surprise.

It couldn't be. She had to be mistaken. It was impossible. Her mind was playing tricks on her. There was no other reasonable explanation.

Concerned, Kelly moved beside her. "Are you alright?"

"Yes," Aurora managed. "I just saw. I mean, I thought I saw." She shook her head to clear it of cobwebs. "Sorry. My mind is playing tricks on me."

"What do you think you saw?"

Before answering, Aurora raised her camera and peered through it searching for her last sight. Nothing. Pulling the camera away from her, she turned back to Kelly. "I thought I saw…" She was going to say Chase, but that was impossible. The whole thing was impossible. How could Chase be over there? How could he be staring at her as if he knew she was watching him through the high-powered lens? "A person," she concluded, feeling it was the safer choice.

"Oh. Probably one of the Lakota."

"Excuse me?"

"They're having an important pow-wow and are utilizing the land. You probably saw a couple of them moving over there, setting up. The event will start tomorrow and last for a couple of days."

"What about the wild horses?"

"The Lakota or others won't bother them, and the horses will still have plenty of space. They'll only be encroaching on a corner section of the land."

Aurora looked toward where she would've sworn she saw Chase's amber eyes gazing at her. At least she wasn't going crazy, thinking so much about him that she was imagining him out of thin air. Probably just caught her so off guard she thought she saw his features on some other male who was only similar in appearance. In her mind, that made sense.

"Do they have events here often?" she asked, making her way back to the truck and climbing in.

"No. Not a private one, at any rate, and not out here. This is the first I'm aware of in the last fifty years or so."

"Any particular reason why they are here this time?"

Kelly shrugged as she headed back towards the offices and gift shop where they'd started. "It's all their land to begin with. Stolen from them when the gold rush started. They've considered this land very sacred, so holding an important religious ceremony around here seems relatively normal. I find it more surprising they aren't out here more often. However, from what I understand, this is going to be unusually large, and therefore probably aren't doing it often due to the amount of work involved in planning the event."

"That makes sense." Still, Aurora couldn't help

but wonder if Chase would be a part of the pow-wow instead of going directly home, especially since he did mention he had some obligations. Maybe this was what he meant, but the idea it was Chase's eyes she had seen staring back at her through her camera lens just didn't seem logical. It was as if he knew she was there, as if he could see her, which, considering the distance, just wasn't possible.

The only thing that made any semblance of her discombobulation was she'd been thinking of Chase so much, she just imagined him, remembering his piercing amber eyes staring into hers.

She'd known from the start it was only going to be a one-night encounter. Hell, that was pretty much all she wanted from him. She'd had enough of relationships and all the bull they usually entailed. An abusive boyfriend, then a neglectful one. Finally, one who was lazy, expecting her to take care of him. Men were good for two things: opening a jar and satisfying a need, and for the most part she could buy a jar opener and a battery-operated satisfier. Yet, Chase was different. He was kind, thoughtful, and oh, so manly. Rugged, tough and yet gentle to her. And satisfy? She still hurt, even when she wasn't moving. He'd found muscles she hadn't even known she'd had.

She couldn't forget him even if she wanted to. And her mind continued to flash back to the very early morning activities. She felt no matter how many hours they'd been together it wasn't going to be enough. And that was the plausible explanation for her mind playing tricks on her.

Chapter Seven

Back at the Franklin, Aurora felt closed in. No matter how much she tried, there wasn't a place in that room she could look and not think of Chase.

Dropping off her extra camera equipment and keeping only her bare camera, she headed out for dinner. Maybe she'd do some gambling and shopping as well. Anything to occupy her mind and keep her loins from burning in need.

Walking along Main Street, she kept looking for something to appease her appetite. It didn't help that Deadwood's facilities were so small. Everywhere she walked, she was reminded of Chase, especially the restaurant Mustang Sally's. It was only when she came across the Fairmont Hotel did things take a promising turn. A hawker trying to get a few more passersby to join the ghost tour of the hotel caught her interest.

At first, Aurora wasn't interested, but anything to help take her mind off Chase was preferable. Although it was probably hokey, it was something to do and she might enjoy hearing the horrors of old

Deadwood. Once she paid for the tour, she was ushered into the bar to wait for the guide to begin. She remembered passing the bar on the walk to her hotel from Mustang Sally's. Was that only two nights ago? She remembered this one in particular because she'd felt a bit light-headed as they were passing it and Chase had offered to buy her another drink and rest. She'd refused the drink, feeling it was all the previous ones catching up to her.

An older man, short, thin, with a huge mustache that curled at the ends in handlebars, caught the group's attention. "Welcome. Welcome. I'm Jed, your guide. You have entered the Historic Fairmont Hotel and all its mysteries, but as you will soon learn, there are more dark secrets than you may care to know. We're considered to be one of the most haunted buildings in Deadwood, and with good reason. Follow me and I'll give you the details on all the grisly aspects of Deadwood and the Badlands.

"In case you've watched the HBO show *Deadwood* or the movie, let me start by saying that the show combined reality and fantasy. I'm going to give you the down-and-dirty truth. I would also like to caution you to watch where you're walking. The hotel itself has been closed for several years and, although the owner is trying to refurbish it, the ghosts aren't really letting him. They like to move the workmen's tools, and some of the men have gotten some experiences so frightening they left and refuse to return. As you can imagine, it's difficult to keep the project constantly going. As a result, we'll be walking by some areas that are not well-maintained or are even in complete disrepair. Please don't go anywhere outside of our tour area and stay with the group. Pictures are encouraged and welcomed. You'll never know when one of our resident ghosts choose to pose for a picture, especially when you least expect it. Let's begin on the second floor as we enter the hotel proper."

Aurora held back slightly, letting the others go ahead. They were only a small group of seven. One couple with two pre-teen children who giggled excitedly in hopes of seeing an apparition and a couple of guys dressed in western clothing with hats bigger than their heads. She guessed they were in their mid-twenties or so. She was the last to follow the group up the creaky stairs with the worn carpeting.

From what was left of the lobby, she could tell it had once been an opulent building. Although in serious need of renovating, the beautiful carved wood reception desk and mailboxes behind it were stunning. Bits of marble peeked through the floor and there were some tarnished gold decorations in the upper ceiling corners. An old player piano sat near the staircase, the wood slightly warped, some keys missing and a cobweb clinging to one corner.

As she slowly ascended, she could swear she heard piano music. It was a startling sound, although very soft. She looked down and realized it was probably a small speaker in the piano for effect. No one else seemed to be bothered by it, or even acknowledge it, so Aurora also ignored it.

This really wasn't her cup of tea, for the most part, and though she didn't believe in ghosts, she was interested in history and architecture. When would she ever have the chance again to see such a historic building as it once was without being modernized or renovated? She was sure the stories would be astounding, if only the walls could talk. But, despite that, she was positive Jed would regale the group with embellished tales of old. Besides, the walking would help her still-sore muscles work through their achiness.

Jed stopped on the second floor landing, waiting patiently until they were all gathered around him.

"I'd like to start by giving you a general history of this old gal. She was built in 1876 as the Melodian. Now, I have to tell you, the Melodian had a bad reputation, almost as bad as Al Swearingen's place, the Gem, which was originally across the street.

"Al's influence in this part of town was so strong he literally ran it, able to keep Seth Bullock and the law away. The area this building is located in was once known as the Badlands. It was an area of prostitution, gambling, being robbed or even murdered, and the law did or could do nothing to stop it. The miners would come to the Badlands in order to enjoy a hot bath, food and the company of one of the many painted ladies, as they were known. However, in most cases, the miners were knocked out and robbed of everything they had, sometimes beaten very severely and left for dead.

"Now most of the women employed in the Badlands came of their own free will, knowing what work would be required of them. Some, however, were told lies, enticing them to come to the area. Al was a great one for that. He'd go on trips to the east and promise girls he thought were pretty and didn't have any ties to come to Deadwood and be a part of his theater as a singer or dancer or even as a server, but once they arrived off the stagecoach he'd force the women into prostitution. They had nowhere to run, no way to get back east. Traveling by foot alone was far too dangerous due to the Indians that surrounded the areas between here and civilization.

"Most were brow-beaten or abused in order to comply and eventually they did. Those that came of their own free will and knew what to expect became some of the wealthiest well-known madams in the area. Each place would try and out-lavish the other to get the miners and other men to attend their establishment.

"In some cases, Al and his goons couldn't tame a wild one, so he'd sell them off to the highest bidder to deal with. Many were bought by the owners of the Melodian. Their fate was horrific if they continued refusing to conform. Punishment would consist of being stripped naked and forced to walk down the stairs we just came up, through the lobby and bar and into the basement cellar. There they'd be chained to the wall and left without food, water, or sanitation, being used by the proprietors of the Melodian as they were broken in. Many of the women didn't survive, and those that did were barely recognizable from the human woman brought in weeks before.

"I'll be talking about one such woman later.

For now, I'd like to tell you about the miner known as Hans Stewart, who is said to haunt these stairs. Hans had found quite of bit of gold dust after working his claim for several months. It was the first time in a couple of years when he came into town to spend time and money on anything more than stocking up on supplies. Seems when he was in the store purchasing his goods, he saw a woman whom he thought was the most beautiful thing he'd ever seen. He told the store clerk to watch his items and he'd be back to collect them later. He followed the woman to the Melodian. Turns out she was one of the painted ladies. He had to be with her, he was so enamored. When she led him up to her room, it's said she turned and pushed him down the stairs, then rushed to his side to steal all his money and gold dust. She had the bouncers take him out back and dump his body while the three then split the loot. Although he was still alive after his fall, albeit badly bruised, the goons took him out back and beat him to death, leaving his body behind the building in the wooded area that existed back then. It's said

Hans comes up these stairs looking for the woman that caught his eye all those years ago." Jeb paused for dramatic effect while the pre-teen boy snapped pictures on his phone as he looked around wide eyed.

"The Melodian only lasted for a year and closed in 1877. I'll tell you why later. In 1879, Deadwood had a major fire. The Melodian, as well as most of Deadwood, burned to the ground. The building was then rebuilt as the Mansion, with famous Turkish baths in the basement. But it, too, didn't last. Another fire in 1894 again destroyed the majority of Deadwood. In 1895, the Fairmont Hotel was built as she stands today. In 1989, the current owner, Ron Russo, purchased the property. It was when he started the major renovations in 1995 that the spirit activity really increased. I'll tell you about the ghost he was visited by when we see the third floor room where he stayed at the time. Shall we continue?" Jeb didn't wait for an answer as he turned and continued down the hallway.

Most of the rooms they passed were as

dilapidated as the lobby. Sadly, there wasn't much left of interest for Aurora to take pictures of as they were mostly stripped bare with nothing more than dull wooden floors and peeling, dingy wallpaper, although that seem to stop the teenagers who were snapping pictures left and right and exclaiming over all the orbs they were able to catch.

She listened to the other stories as she sadly looked around as they walked. There was no electricity, so when the light from outside dimmed, Jeb gave them all battery operated lanterns to carry. She couldn't help but sympathize with those who lived here so long ago. Their lives were hard and so sad it wasn't a surprise why they continued to haunt the building.

By the time they moved to the third floor, Aurora had caught some of their enthusiasm, snapping a few pictures with her camera to see if she could catch a ghost. They entered one room furnished with some pictures on the walls, a small bed with a threadbare red bedspread, and a half-dressed mannequin positioned in a semi-sitting position. Jed waited until they all gathered within the room before he began speaking.

"You might remember I mentioned Ron Russo staying in one of the rooms up here when he started renovations on the Fairmont back in 1995. He chose the room of Margaret Brown, also known as Maggie. She was described as a woman with brilliant red hair. Ron awoke one night and saw a red-haired apparition wearing a long green dress. It was only upon investigating the background of the hotel did he learn about Maggie, who jumped out of the window and landed in the alley below. Only it had been raining and the newspapers claim she fell in a muddy area. As a result, it took three days for her to die from her injuries. The story is she might've been pregnant and told her boyfriend she was going to have their baby. The boyfriend became very upset and the two had a huge fight. He left her and she became so depressed she began drinking heavily. The news reported she had been maintaining cups prior to her suicide. That's a term meaning she was drinking. Unable to live without him, she stood on the window sill, faced the room and jumped out backwards."

Jed paused a few moments before he led them back into the hallway. "You might capture a picture of the Grumpy Man. A few years ago, we had the television show *The Dead Files* here and the medium, Amy, gave us information about the man in a cowboy hat that several people had encounters with prior to their investigation. Doing some background research, we think the Grumpy Man is a man named Henry who's still angry over his prostitute girlfriend dying of syphilis."

Jeb took them inside a corner room and waited. "This will be our final stop on the tour and I'd like to take this moment to thank you all for joining me. Once we get back to the bar where we began, I'll tell you one more story. For now, let me tell you about the last room we will visit while here in the hotel proper." He set his lantern down and sighed as he looked about the room. "This room is my favorite and the saddest, to me. If you remember when we started, I mentioned that Al Swearingen would go out east to entice women to come to his establishment under false pretenses. I also mentioned I'd be talking about one of the girls that came as a result of his promises, but because she chose to fight against the work they gave her and the resulting beatings she took to try and subdue her, break her, and they eventually sold her to the Melodian.

"Her name was Lily-Anne Clovis. She was born in Missouri, fell in love and married a preacher man. Unfortunately, he became ill and died. Al was just passing through on his return to Deadwood with a couple of other girls he'd found around Chicago and asked her to join them. He promised her employment as a server in the Gem Theater, with room and boarding with the other girls. He enticed her with the opportunity to start a new life with a financial means to do so, as well as an opportunity to get away from her sad memories."

Those last words made Aurora shiver, as she'd only taken this tour to get away from her memories. How ironic, she thought.

"I can only imagine how a god-fearing woman, still suffering the loss of her husband and hoping for the promises Al made for a new lease on life, might feel when she realized she'd been thrown into the depths of wicked depravity. She had no money, no way to return home, nowhere else in town to go, for no one would go against Al with any of the girls he brought to service the men of Deadwood.

"It's said, shortly after she arrived, she was beaten into submission and Al did most of the injuries himself. When he tried to take her to his bed a couple of weeks after her arrival, she fought so hard that he decided she wasn't worth the effort to deal with her. He sold her to the Melodian, who didn't even bother to pretend to rehabilitate her. Instead they immediately threw her down in the hole, chaining her to the cold walls. The few times they did visit her in the following days, they would beat her or take her in front of the other women.

"Then, after being in the hole for a couple of weeks, starving, dirty, smelly from her own bodily fluids and weak from all the punishments she'd endured, one of the managers, Pierre Hills, brought her up to this room. He dumped her in a tub of water to clean her up, brought some food for her, but only let her have a couple of bites before pushing the food out of her reach. He then," Jeb looked at the two youngest on the tour, obviously trying to think of a polite way to continue, "had physical relations with her. However, she continued to fight him, even in her weakened state. Unfortunately, there were men at the time who enjoyed carnal pleasures not otherwise socially accepted. There were a few brothels that allowed men like them to do as they pleased for an extra fee. Pierre was one of those who enjoyed asphyxiating the girls he was with. However, he knew he couldn't go as far as killing them, only cutting off their air temporarily. But, with Lily-Anne, he was over-exuberant or she was far more fragile than he expected, no one really knows for sure. What we do know is, during their act, he killed her. Not wanting to be caught and forced to abide Al's law, he staged her murder by throwing her out the window, claiming it was a suicide.

"At first, no one argued with him. They all knew how rebellious she was. After all, Al sold her just weeks prior, so it seemed obvious that the first chance she'd had to escape, she took it, even if it meant throwing herself out of a third-story window."

"Did they ever realize she didn't commit suicide?" the mother asked.

Jeb nodded. "Yes. When the doctor examined her body, he realized her neck was broken and there were fingerprint bruises. Since Pierre was the only man in the room, they knew he was the culprit, even though he tried to finagle his way out of the charge. He bribed a couple of locals to vouch for him, saying he'd come down for a drink when she jumped from the building, but no one believed the locals. Al had him dragged from the building and lynched in the middle of the street as a warning to all those who came to the Badlands that he was the one who ruled the roost and his law would be the law in that part of Deadwood. Pierre cursed Al and the town, saying he'd never leave, but that death would be the door to more killings in the Badlands. Although there were many deaths, it was no more so than to be expected for the area run by Swearingen. However, it's said that Pierre's lynching was why the Melodian was shut down in 1877, a little less than two years before the first major fire in the town."

Aurora shivered, a cold chill seeping into her very bones at the gruesome story. She was actually surprised she didn't see her breath as she exhaled. She hadn't realized during the telling of the story her hand had clutched her throat.

Jeb led them out of the room and down the back stairs.

As Aurora inhaled another breath of cold air, she coughed, needing to hold back until the hacking fit subsided before moving to catch up to the rest of the group. Even then, she felt a bit light-headed from the lack of oxygen as a result of coughing so hard.

In moments, she'd caught up to the group just

entering the bar where they'd started. They stood in the corner and turned in their lanterns.

"Our last story is what occurred next door at the famous Saloon Number 10. The infamous murder of Wild Bill Hickok by Jack McCall. Although there are no reported hauntings of Hickok himself, Jack is said to still visit the bar."

Aurora barely heard the rest of the story. Although the coughing had subsided, she continued to find it difficult to breathe and the dizziness increased. She felt like she was drunk and hadn't even had one drink yet. She moved around the small group to the bar and ordered a whiskey, her hand shaking as she brought the amber liquid to her lips. She hoped the concoction burning its way down her throat and into her belly would help with the light-headedness as well as the coldness she still seemed to be suffering from. However, it only seemed to make her symptoms worse.

A buzzing in her head, a ringing in her ears, and everything began to grow dark, the sounds and smells of the bar fading into nothingness.

Chapter Eight

Aurora's eyes fluttered open to see dozens of people standing over her.

"Step back."

"Give her air."

"Move away."

"Let me in."

"Paramedics are here. Outta the way."

Trying to wave off everyone, Aurora spoke hoarsely. "I'm okay."

"Let us check anyways." The emergency medical technicians cleared a space around her as they knelt beside her checking her vitals and asking her questions like who she was and if she knew where she was.

She answered all of them correctly as she waited for the prodding and poking they were doing to subside.

"Have you eaten?" the oldest looking technician asked.

Aurora thought about it for a moment, frowning. "Actually, I can't remember having anything today."

"Your blood sugar is a bit low. We can take you to the hospital to be checked out completely, if you wish."

"No, thank you. I'll get something to eat immediately. I'm sure I'll be fine with some food in my stomach. I feel better even now."

The older man frowned. "Are you sure? Just to be checked out? Just to be safe?"

Suddenly, Aurora realized they thought she might be intoxicated and smiled sweetly at them. "I'm sure. I don't remember eating and the day has been so full of activities that I just didn't realize it. And I was just on the ghost tour. Lots of stairs. When we came back down, I had a shot of whiskey and I think it was just too much for my system to handle. I'm very sorry. I didn't mean to cause any problems."

The older man, obviously in charge, nodded. "We'll need you to sign a release form indicating you refused transportation to the hospital for further evaluation."

"Of course. My pleasure." Aurora got to her feet, one of the younger men assisting her. They handed her the paperwork, which she signed, then followed them outside, not wanting to continue being the focus of so many prying eyes.

Once free from the paramedics, Jed approached her. "Are you sure you're okay?"

"Yes. Sorry about causing such a fuss and interrupting your tour."

"It was the end of it, so don't worry any." He shuffled his feet slightly. "Do you mind if I ask you a personal question?"

She frowned. "I guess it'll be okay."

"What did you mean by 'he's free.'?"

Aurora gave him a perplexed looked. "Excuse me?"

"You said that just as you passed out. I was wondering who you were referring to."

She thought about it for a moment, then shrugged her shoulders. "No clue. The only guys I know left town last night or early this morning."

"Are you sure there is nothing else we can do

for you?"

Aurora shook her head. "No, thank you." She dug into her purse and pulled out a couple of dollars, handing him the tip. "It was a great tour despite the auspicious ending. Thank you."

Jed took the money, slipping it quickly into his pants pocket. "Thanks."

Aurora quickly scurried down the block, ducking into the steakhouse that was part of her hotel. It was best she eat something immediately, and if she were recognized, she could always take the food up to her room where she could dine in private.

Thankfully, though, she didn't recognize anyone and they didn't seem to notice her. As she enjoyed her meal, her thoughts returned to what Kelly had informed her about the pow-wow. Maybe she really did see Chase, although how he was watching her was inconceivable. However, the pow-wow was supposed to be a huge event with various bands and maybe even tribes coming from all over to attend.

The more she thought about it, the more she knew she had to go. Maybe, just maybe she'd even get the opportunity to see Chase once again. Even if from afar. Plus, the pictures would be phenomenal for such a once-in-a-lifetime event. She remembered Kelly stating it wouldn't be open to the public, so she'd have to be stealthy, but the idea wormed its way into her soul and she knew it was what she was going to do the following day.

With a plan formulated, she finished her dinner and headed back to her room. It was still early in the evening for her and she wanted to get some work done from the multitude of photographs she'd taken earlier that day. She was, therefore, surprised to find some detectives waiting for her in the lobby.

Both of them showed their badges as they approached her.

"Ms. Taylor?" the older of the two asked softly, so as not to draw too much attention from the gamblers nearby.

"Yes?" She looked at both of them wondering if they were here because she passed out earlier.

"Is there someplace we can talk?" The younger one moved closer so he could talk more quietly.

She looked around nervously.

"We're with the Deadwood Police. We have some questions we'd like to ask you. Would you mind following us?"

"Where? What kind of questions?"

"The hotel is letting us use one of their conference rooms. This is Detective Sean Collins and I'm Detective Joe Hansley. We'd like to speak with you about an incident that occurred just a couple of doors from the room you're staying in. You gave your information to Officer Perry yesterday?"

"That's correct. I did. Sure. I can answer questions, though I doubt I'll be much help."

"Follow me, please." Joe turned and led the way past the slot machines, down a hall and into a back room. There were a couple of other uniformed officers standing nearby, which eased Aurora from thinking it might have been a trick to lure her into a spot to kill her, like they had that woman.

"Would you like some coffee or water?" Sean indicated the seat she was to take.

"No, thank you. I just had dinner."

"Good. Then we'll just begin." Joe took a seat, pulling a pad of paper and pen to him to make his notes upon. He seemed to be in charge of the interview. "Do you know an Allison Harper?"

Aurora frowned, pulling her camera closer. "Um. I met an Allison a couple of nights ago, but I don't know her last name."

Sean opened a folder and took out a picture of her, shoving the photograph towards her. Nervously, Aurora peered at it. It was a dead woman, and although the face was pale with slightly bluish lips, she recognized the woman immediately and sat back. "Yes, that's the woman I met."

"What do you know about her?"

Shaking her head, Aurora shrugged slightly. "Not much. We only had a brief conversation on the porch. She mentioned she came to watch the cowboys in the PBR and that she was from

Bismarck, North Dakota."

"Did you see her with anyone else?"

"No. Sorry."

"What about later?"

"Later? As I said I only saw her for a few minutes on the porch before she called it a night and went to her room."

"Did you follow her there?"

"No. I didn't even know what room she was in."

Joe frowned and nodded to Sean who took the photo away and replaced it with another. "Care to explain this then?"

Aurora paled when she saw it.

"It was taken from the hall cameras," Joe added quietly as he watched her reaction and body language.

She looked up at the two detectives, wide eyed and in shock. "I don't know. I can't explain it. I mean…wait. I remember. I wasn't sleeping well that night and I was sleepwalking."

Sean snorted. "Sleepwalking, really? Into

another person's room?"

"Honestly. Surely, those same cameras will show that I headed downstairs after I tried to get back in my room. I needed to get another key."

"Were you sleepwalking then?"

"No. I woke up and found myself in the hallway."

"Have you been diagnosed with this affliction before?"

"Actually, no. As far as I know, I've never done it before."

"Why do you think it occurred now?"

At least Joe seemed to be speaking to her as if he believed her, even if only minutely.

"I was having some personal issues that day. A lot of stress, confusion. But I swear, I don't remember going to visit Allison that night. I don't own a gun nor carry a knife."

"How do you think she was killed?" Joe furrowed his brow.

She shrugged. "Honestly, I don't know."

"She was strangled. From behind. With a

drapery tie."

"Oh." So much for her not being physically able to kill someone without a weapon. "I didn't know her. Why would I kill her?"

"That's what we want to know. Why did you visit her?"

"I didn't. At least I don't remember doing so." She looked at the picture again showing her in front of Allison's door.

"Sleepwalking. Yes, you said."

"I'm not lying. Ask the front desk. When I got the new key, I told them I locked myself out by sleepwalking."

"Rather convenient, don't you think?" Sean was the hothead one of the two of them.

She took a deep breath as she sat back. "Convenient, maybe. The truth? Entirely."

"The hotel states your reservation shows you checking out of the hotel tomorrow?"

"Yes."

"We ask that you stay around for a couple more days."

"Are you charging me with something?"

"Not yet," Sean ominously stated.

Joe stood. "It's more a convenience in case we have more questions."

"I'll extend my hotel room for two more days, but then I really need to get back to St. Louis."

Joe nodded. "We have all your information. I'll let you know if we will need you again or not as soon as we finish our interviews."

"I hope you find the real culprit. I've been a bit nervous staying here as a result. As a matter of fact, would you mind if someone escorts me to my room?"

"We can do that." Joe opened the conference room door, instructing Officer Perry to escort Aurora to her quarters.

Glad to be back in the safety of her room, she plopped on the bed, her mind whirling from the questions the detectives posed. She certainly didn't blame them for wanting to talk to her, but there was no way she'd kill anyone, least of all a stranger. Why would she? But then, why would she be sleepwalking either? She'd doubt her alibi too, if she was them. However, giving her the extra couple of days reinforced her decision to visit the private pow-wow. How could she not?

Chapter Nine

At first, Aurora wasn't sure she was in the right location, even if it was extremely early in the morning. There weren't many vehicles around that she could see and assumed there must be another area in which they parked. As a result, her car would be too noticeable. However, she knew this was the sight she'd seen from the hills on the other side of the river and Wild Horse Sanctuary. The lack of vehicles made her wonder, but the firelights, chanting, talking, as well as the sound of drums, indicated otherwise. She discovered a location she could hide her car, surrounded by several trees, allowing her to move around a bit without being seen. At least that's what she hoped.

There wasn't a whole lot of cover between her parked car and the main event, but she'd gone with black clothing and did her best to stay within the shadows of the trees and boulders as cover. She'd managed a vantage point and settled in as the Lakota hustled and bustled about below.

Thankfully, there was so much activity setting

up tipis and tents, she was able to get her spot without giving a single thought to the snakes that might be around. She had a silencer on her camera and a black sweater to help keep her warm. She'd have to wait until others left or fell asleep before she could make her way out of the area again, but the anticipation of the pictures she'd achieve outweighed any other concerns she might otherwise have, as well as the hopeful promise of seeing Chase, even from a distance.

Aurora's heart raced with nervous excitement. She knew this pow-wow was forbidden to outsider eyes, which made it all the more enticing for her. There were so many people, each with various colors, banners and ornamental displays; she was highly impressed, knowing this was where she should be. He'd kill her if he knew she were here, but still, thoughts and aches from the previous evening, as well as the clothing, painted and decorated horses, the sights and sounds of the whole event, made everything fascinating to her.

It was obvious everyone there wasn't Sioux.

There were some elaborate headdresses, while others wore feathers or braids. Some were clean shaven. Some of them were dressed from head to toe in bright designs, while others were naked with the exception of well-placed cloths. Some were heavily painted from head to foot and others were just minimally so, if at all. The variance in clothing styles, decorations, whether or not they used paints or feathers or even furs were vastly different to be a single tribal nation.

Aurora couldn't believe how lucky she was to have learned about the event. To say it was resplendent would be an understatement, and she was pretty positive no one outside of one of the tribes represented here has seen anything quite like it. She couldn't remember taking so many pictures before. She'd already gone through one SD card and was close to filling up another. She only had one other totally empty with her and berated herself for not bringing more. How could she have known though? She wasn't even sure she would be able to secure a hiding spot to her advantage.

She'd gotten hundreds of shots, changing the SD card for the second time. She tucked the used one in her pocket, as she had the first one. Picking up her camera for a couple more shots, her vision through the lens was soon blocked.

"What the fuck do you think you're doing here?"

She knew from the voice exactly who it was. Slowly, guiltily, she pulled her camera down and gazed into the angry face of Chase. His hair was loose, a feather stuck haphazardly on one side, and he wore breeches under a heavily decorated loin cloth. His chest was covered by an open buckskinned shirt.

He was furious. His stance with legs apart, arms folded over his broad bare chest, his face red with his anger, his jaw clenched, Aurora knew she might be in some serious trouble.

He gripped her firmly, pulling her roughly to her feet. "You've no idea what you've done," he said through clenched teeth.

"I'm sorry. I was just so curious."

"Your curiosity is determined to get you killed. Stop being the fucking cat." Chase bent down, scooping up her camera equipment.

While he looked away, she moved one of the used SD cards into her bra for safer keeping. It was all she had time for. As he turned back around, he started to drag her out of the area in angry silence.

She knew she'd committed a grievous sin and she was ashamed, but not enough to possibly give up the pictures she'd taken.

"What's *she* doing here? Why aren't you taking her down to the council?" Brandon startled them both as he seemingly appeared out of nowhere.

Chase took on a guilty look and Aurora instantly knew he'd been trying to get her out before anyone caught on she'd been there.

Brandon obviously knew it too, for even though he'd lowered his voice, the anger and contempt were quite explicit. "You were going to sneak her back out? What the fuck is wrong with you? You know the rules better than anyone, yet you're making an exception for her?" He literally spat the last two words at them.

Chase pushed Aurora behind him. Old laws would require her death for her spying and intrusion. Times had changed but had his band? He hadn't wanted to take the chance. He couldn't. There was something about Aurora he couldn't resist, but he knew Brandon and, despite their extremely long friendship, Brandon wasn't about to let him help her escape.

"Get back, Brandon. This has nothing to do with you."

"Nothing, bro? You'd better look around. She's seen us and probably has all the evidence on her camera. You know the laws. No exception. She's going in front of the elders. If you don't bring her, I will."

"You won't touch her." Chase growled, low and almost inhuman.

Brandon shoved him and reached for Aurora, but Chase recovered quickly and slugged Brandon so hard he fell.

Aurora gasped loudly. What had she done?

These two were childhood friends, fighting because of her!

Brandon sprung to his feet then leapt at Chase, transforming almost immediately into a mountain lion, pouncing on him.

Aurora couldn't help but scream and rub her eyes. This couldn't be real!

The cougar and man rolled around. The former using claws and teeth while Chase continued punching the animal with all his strength. In moments that seemed to last an eternity, they were surrounded by many people.

"Enough!" A booming voice broke through the melee. Chase and Brandon stopped immediately as the lion transformed once again into the man Aurora knew as Brandon.

Aurora shook her head at the impossible. "Oh my god! What? He? Cougar!" She couldn't complete a sentence, much less a coherent thought, but at least she'd stopped screaming. "Did you see that? A cougar? He was a man! And he…he changed! A man can't do that? Did you see that?

It's impossible! Oh my god! What just happened?"

Chase knew he had to do something to get her to be quiet, although he understood how strange and disconcerting everything was. Brandon shifting in front of her sealed her fate and his heart sank. He should've known better when he saw her peering down at him through her camera yesterday. He should've gone to see her and tell her to stay away, but he'd been warned to let her go and he knew it'd be nigh on impossible to leave her again. He could still smell her on his body, still hear her cries of pleasure. The memory had haunted him and it had taken all his willpower to focus on today's event preparations.

He reached out to pull her to him in hopes of calming her, but she pushed him away in fear. He didn't think he could hurt any more than he had when Brandon discovered her, but knowing she was terrified of him tore him up inside. He hated the idea she feared him and wanted desperately to take his hurtful frustrations out on Brandon.

He hadn't cared Brandon had clawed and bit

him. He'd heal, and quickly enough as part of his special gifts. Although he could've shifted and trampled Brandon, he hadn't wanted to scare her any more than she already was. He could pummel Brandon for his thoughtlessness, and he hoped that's what it was, because if Brandon had shifted in front of her on purpose to secure her punishment, Chase would kill him.

Aurora might've had a chance without learning who and what there were. He'd look at her pictures, then erase them all after he saw what, if any damage had been done. He could've salvaged everything if Brandon hadn't screwed it all up.

"What's the meaning?" The man who'd yelled 'enough' spoke to Aurora, who was still stupefied.

"What? What's the meaning? WHAT'S the MEANING?" Her voice went up an octave with each sentence. "What's the meaning of...of..." She waved her wrist, her palm pointing towards Brandon, her eyes still wide with fear. "He! He changed! Mountain lion!" She was back to single syllables again. "Didn't you all see him do that?"

Chase stepped up to the man known as Standing Bear. "I know her. She's overly curious. Yesterday, she was taking pictures of the horses at the Sanctuary for calendars to help raise money for their cause. She saw me though her camera, probably got curious and, learning about an event, decided to check it out."

"She's the one?"

"Yes, sir."

Standing Bear frowned and walked around her. Chase noticed the men move aside as Zonta appeared with Mahkah and Mato on each of her sides, followed by Kyle. The men stood back as Zonta approached Aurora and took several deep breaths, her eyes narrowing with each one. Chase felt sick. He knew his scent was on Aurora, just as hers had lingered on him since they'd been intimately joined. At least Aurora had stopped jabbering almost incoherently.

Zonta stepped back and whispered something to Standing Bear, who growled unhappily. "Bring her to Chase's compound and keep her inside and under guard until I speak with the rest of the council to determine our next steps."

Standing Bear, Zonta, Mahkeh and Mato left while the rest of the group surrounding Chase and Aurora funneled them towards the encampment.

Chase took her elbow, even though she tried to pull away, and led her to his tipi. His grip tightened, so she brooked no further argument in resisting and remained quiet as they walked.

When they arrived, the others waited outside while Chase and Aurora entered. He only released her once inside.

Chapter Ten

"What the hell, Aurora. Do you have any idea what you've done? I can't get you out of this. I can't save you." He was exasperated and he paced the small area, his hand running though his hair in his distress.

"Save me? From what? What's going on? Brandon? Kyle? *You?*"

He sighed and turned to face her. "Yes. Me too. All of us here. But, not a cougar. We are each different. And save you from a death sentence. We don't take kindly to outsiders knowing about us and what we are. What we can do."

"Stop scaring the poor girl. There are exceptions to every rule." A feminine lilting voice stated as three women entered the tent.

The one who spoke nodded towards the flap. "Go. The elders want to see you and we'll stay with her."

Without waiting for an answer or response, Hope moved past him to Aurora. "Hi. I'm Hope and I'm mostly human. I know you're a bit freaked, but let us help. Okay?"

The second woman stepped up. "You're Aurora. Pretty name. I'm Sierra. From Peoria, Illinois originally. Sit with us and let us answer the billions of questions you must have. That's Feather. She's one of them. Comanche, but don't mind her."

Aurora peered at Hope and Sierra, both obviously non-Natives with their light complexions, and then at Feather, who was by the door and obviously very pregnant. Aurora calmed down, realizing Chase was no longer there and maybe the nightmare would be over soon.

"Can you please tell me what *Twilight Zone* I just entered? Did I see, really see, what I thought I saw?" Her voice faded in uncertainly. Maybe she'd finally flipped and should be admitted to an insane asylum.

"Yes. You did. It's okay, though. They all have special gifts." Hope sat in front of the fire and patted a couple of blankets next to her, indicating for Aurora to sit down.

Sierra sat on the other side of Hope while

Feather took a place by the flap, her hand on her rotund belly, rubbing it softly.

After a few uncertain minutes, Aurora sat down.

Sierra smiled. "It's going to be okay. There are several who won't allow them to kill you, including Zonta."

"Zonta?"

"Yeah. She's the older woman you saw with Standing Bear. The female who sniffed you? She's a shaman, what you might call a prophet. Her name means honest and trustworthy and she's a very fair person."

"Slower, Hope," Sierra admonished. "It's a lot to take in all at once." She turned to Aurora. "It's okay. You're having a normal reaction to being freaked out. You should've seen me. I actually traveled back in time and didn't even realize it to meet my husband, Stone. Talk about being freaked and disbelieving. Here I am waving my cell phone around like some idiot wondering why I couldn't get any service." Sierra pantomimed the movements causing Aurora to smile, then give a small chuckle. Even Feather snickered softly at her antics. Sierra noticed Aurora appeared calmer and more relaxed as she rested her hands in her lap.

"I was kidnapped by Raven's tribe because they thought I already knew what he was. When he finally told me, I thought it was a colossal joke, and then he shifted and I freaked like you did. And like you, my life was on the line." Hope patted Aurora's hand.

"Shifted?" Aurora was more serene, her brain starting to work and become inquisitive.

"That's what it's called when they change from human to their spirit animal form," Hope responded, unsure how much Aurora knew or didn't and what she should tell her.

"One band in every tribe has this gift," Feather spoke from her post. "Because we were willing to sacrifice ourselves for the good of our people."

"Instead of their actual sacrifice, their God stopped them, and in return for their attempt at selflessness they were given the gift of being able to shift into their spirit guide. They also have other gifts, like longevity and healing ability. They recoup much faster than us mere humans."

"That explains the sixteen times. What is Chase?"

"Sixteen times? Lakota."

Aurora rolled her eyes. "Never mind. I know he's Lakota. But…?"

"Each is different. I don't know," Hope responded, looking at the other two to see if they might know, but neither of them spoke up.

"Chase is unique, powerful," Feather called from her spot.

"Ah." Hope added to Aurora, "That means he has more than one spirit guide and therefore able to take additional forms. There aren't too many who are that powerful."

"But you don't know what he, I mean, what they are?" Aurora directed her question to Feather.

Feather paused, then shrugged. "He should be the one to tell you."

Aurora raised her eyebrows at that statement,

but didn't have anything further to say. Would Chase even talk to her after this? After the way she pulled away from him?

Feather struggled to her feet. "They're coming."

Everyone else stood, Hope patting Aurora on the arm. "It'll be okay."

Hope, Feather and Sierra exited the tipi as Standing Bear and the other older men entered. Aurora noticed immediately Chase wasn't with them, nor was Zonta, and that made Aurora become anxious once more.

Standing Bear pointed as two of the older men approached. "Bring her." Standing Bear didn't wait, but left while the two other men reached for her.

Aurora waved them off. "I heard. I'm going."

She picked up her step to quickly catch up to Standing Bear. They soon entered a circle of people, all in different dress and different ages. She saw Hope next to a tall man. Sierra was also there, but farther away. She didn't see Feather, but the woman was pregnant after all. Aurora's camera was nearby on a makeshift platform, but she didn't see any sign of Chase.

She frowned when she did notice Brandon there, glaring at her the whole time she came within his view.

She became very self-conscious at everyone staring at her and was grateful when she met Hope's eyes, who smiled at her in encouragement, giving Aurora a sense of assuredness. Still, she couldn't help but wonder where Chase was and how much trouble she might have gotten him into.

Brandon spoke first. "She needs to die. Our old laws call for it."

The man next to Hope stood. "Raven. Ojibwa. There are special circumstances. The old ways aren't always right when they've been chosen. My wife is the perfect example."

"Your wife is an exception." A man near Sierra stood. "But, there are many exceptions. Stone. Cheyanne."

"There's never been a mortal or non-Lakota in our special band," Brandon affirmed. "Just because you have exceptions, doesn't mean we should be so lax in our laws."

Aurora wondered what power he held over the proceedings. Those she knew as the elders sat quietly nearby, watching the crowd intently.

"Raine. Comanche. Then maybe it's time you consider the possibility. It seems senseless to throw two lives away. Induct her into your band. Let the Lakota male have her and she'll keep the secret."

"Renegade. Comanche. As a detective, I question if she is willing to give up her life as she knows it. Is she even aware of everything it entails to join the band? To be with Chase for her life? To even consider combining their life forces? She needs to be informed of all of this for you and her to make a rational decision."

Raven stood again. "She'd marry him. He'd bond closer to the band."

Zonta spoke from behind Aurora, which was why Aurora hadn't seen her. "It would be the most appropriate. She does, after all, carry his child."

"Wait. What?" Aurora had stood quietly as

they had all talked about her as if she weren't even there, but now she couldn't hold her tongue any longer. "I think you're gravely mistaken."

Hope shook her head, indicating Aurora not to speak, but Aurora was beyond caring. True, they'd had unprotected sex, multiple, multiple times, but that was only two days ago. The best tests on Earth couldn't tell if she was pregnant, and even if by some weird miracle she was, that wasn't their decision.

When a quiet descended over the group, she'd heard a movement behind her and turned around to notice Chase enter the circle.

He walked straight up to Aurora and took her hand. This time, she didn't pull away. She did, however, notice all the bandages on his arms, neck and torso. Brandon really did a number on him. She frowned as she contemplated all the damage.

Zonta spoke softly. "He'll give up rodeo and settle in the band as promised. They will marry. She'll bear his child."

Aurora's head snapped around and she pulled

her shaking hand away. "No. Stop making plans for my life. I'm not with child. It's impossible."

"Let them talk. In private," Raven spoke up. "She's a mortal whose life just transformed a thousand-fold. Chase needs to talk to her. Explain things."

Stone nodded. "Give her time to understand what's at stake. Give them some privacy and time. If we keep her here, you don't have to worry about her telling others about us."

The large group surrounding them nodded, except for Brandon who just glared before moving with the rest to other areas in order to give them some privacy. Chase held his hand out for Aurora, but she lifted her chin in refusal.

"Please. Let us talk in my tent?"

She hesitated a moment, then, without his assistance, she walked towards his tipi. Once inside, she paced the small, cramped area. "This is crazy. What's wrong with all of you? Shifting people? Killing outsiders? Telling me I'm pregnant? With your kid, no less. Did you tell them every sordid detail of having sex with me? Tell them what a whore I am for making the moves on you? That I'm so insatiable I kept up with you and your supernatural stamina? No wonder! Your special gifts. Sixteen times! I should've known something was wrong. I wasn't making love to a man. I was having sex with a…with a… Shit. I don't even know what you are."

Chase started to reach for her, but then pulled back. She was ranting, upset. It was a lot to take in. He'd hoped the human women from the other tribes would help, but he could tell Aurora thought he was a monster. An aberration.

When Zonta told him she was carrying his child, he was stunned and realized it was why the prophet told him not to be with her. Why he had to let her go. A complication that had prevented her from simply being chastised, warned and released. Yet in this case, also a fortuitous circumstance, which prevented her immediate demise. Chase shrunk back, letting her alone and not forcing the issue. "I know it's a lot to comprehend. Ask me anything you want to know. I'll tell you everything now."

"Why? Why now?"

"Because despite everything, your curiosity has led you into the world of the forbidden. You know about us. About me. What we are and what we can do. It's a death sentence. Only you being with my child has stayed their hands."

"So, it's true?" She turned to face him incredulously.

He sighed and ran a hand through his hair. "Yes. It's all true."

"You change? Like Brandon?"

"Yes and no."

She gave him a look and he continued.

"Brandon is cougar. I'm bison and hawk."

"How old." She remembered Hope saying they could live a long life.

"Nine hundred thirty-four."

"You're shitting me."

"No. I'm not. I was born in a time before the interlopers, the Europeans came. I've been here since the beginning. Since we made the pact with the Great Mystery. I was part of the decision to sacrifice ourselves when White Calf Woman asked us of it. I've watched the others not of our band suffer. I've watched men change and innovations become born." Chase stood still, staring at the fire, not wanting to frighten or upset her any more than she already was.

"Maybe you should start from the very beginning. I'm having a bit of difficulty comprehending everything."

Chase nodded, pressing his lips together. "I'm only one in the band of special Lakota. One band in each tribe was given an extraordinary gift. The ability to shift into our animal spirits. In the beginning of time, Wakan Tanka, the Great Mystery, sent the White Buffalo Calf Woman to tell the Lakota they were to sacrifice one band for the good of the others. My band discussed it with the elders and we agreed we'd be the ones to give of ourselves for the greater purpose.

After making our final farewells and putting

our meager affairs in order, we set out to the sacred lands to make our ultimate sacrifice—our very lives. When we first arrived, we were surprised to find other bands of various nations already there with a multitude more arriving each day, depending on how far they had to travel. Comanche, Cherokee, Seminole, Iroquois, Ottawa, Ojibwa and several others, too many to name. Despite the animosity between several of the tribes, we all knew why we were there and managed to put our differences aside. We resided in peace as we waited for the attendance of all who were called and the Great Mystery to let us know our time had finally come.

The land was filled with so many people, colors of various nations, tipis of many designs, it was hard to go far without running into another tribal group. However, despite the amount of people, there always seemed to be enough food and fresh water. It amazed even the elders, who declared it was a sign their time had not fully come yet. Those who were not nomadic, but lived in wigwams and other buildings, managed the journey and were given shelter by those of us who could provide it.

Then one day they stopped coming. We knew our final moments had finally arrived in whatever way our culture dictated, but even before the first life was taken, the Great Mystery sent word to the elders that we were all being tested. No one was to sacrifice themselves to prove their worth. Instead we were all given a very rare and unique gift. Each person's spirit guide appeared in front of them and shimmered into our bodies. We all received the abilities to shift into our animal guide and were endowed with the spirit's aptitudes as well as longevity." Chase sat cross-legged in front of the small blaze in the center. "My band and the others that came then now make a pilgrimage once every one hundred years on the anniversary of our transformation to celebrate our gifts and thank the Great Mystery for all he's given us. We rejoice in the peace we share as a result. A peace brought about because of our common sacrifice.

"We met here, on this spot, nine hundred years ago. We sang, we danced. Enemies laid down their weapons. There was nothing to fight for anymore. The others would continue those fights. We were all here for the same purpose. To make peace with ourselves and with others before we all entered the Happy Hunting Grounds of our own accord."

"Still. Nine hundred thirty-four years." She couldn't comprehend any of it. "And your animal spirits are bison and hawk?"

"Yes. In our culture, bison is the sacred symbol embodying life and abundance. The hawk is a symbol of the east and speaks of speed, dedication, courage and strength. These are the two animal spirits that I'm blessed with. Thing is, Aurora, the prophet sees much hidden from the eyes of the rest. As a prophet, she can see more than what is within normal vision or knowledge. If she says you carry my child, you can believe it is the truth."

Aurora shook her head. "No. We only had sex two nights ago. It's not possible to even think of being pregnant. Besides, I'm on birth control."

Chase sighed and ran a hand through his hair. "We were gifted with many blessings. One of them was your diseases and medicines don't affect us. That's how we avoided things like smallpox, influenza, typhoid and other things that killed so many of our people without these gifts. Some of us even had gifts even before the Great Mystery gave us more. Zonta has the gift of sight. To see things that haven't occurred yet. She warned me to stay away from you, but I couldn't. And I tried to stop myself from getting more deeply involved, but I couldn't. When it comes to you, I'm weak. Somehow. For some reason, you call to me and I can't refuse. I'm sorry. All of this is my doing. I can only ask your forgiveness."

"For what? Having sex with me?"

"Making love. You're the temple I worshipped. Look, the bottom line is, you're going to have my child. A predicament you wouldn't be in had I done as Zonta asked. And maybe your curiosity wouldn't have been so heightened if you hadn't seen me yesterday. I sensed you were near and I couldn't help but look for you. The position you're now in, well, it isn't safe. To keep both you and our child protected, you need to marry me."

"Marry you? Oh, you're off your flipping rocker."

"I know I'm probably not what you imagined as a husband, but I'll treat you well. I can take care of you." Chasse lowered his head. She seemed to hate him right now, and he couldn't blame her. It was obvious from the disdain she had over the idea of being her husband. She didn't want him, and his heart ached as he clenched his hands into fists in order to focus on something other than rejection or forcing her to be with him. A feeling he knew all too well.

"At what cost?"

"What do you mean?"

"You stop the PBR?"

"Yes."

"I give up my gallery and my home in St. Louis?"

Chase frowned. "Yes."

"No. Sorry. Ain't gonna happen."

"You don't understand. The only choice is to

marry me or die. Would marrying me be so awful?"

Before she had an opportunity to respond, a loud commotion occurred and Kyle entered.

"You better get out here and bring her with you."

Chase didn't bother with niceties. He took Aurora by the arm and led her back to the inner circle. Several of the men were gathered together talking in rushed, hushed whispers. Several turned, glaring at Aurora as Chase guided her towards the center of the group.

She could tell something changed and it wasn't good.

"What happened?" Chase was also curious to know what all the hubbub was about.

"Jasper was just found dead." Renegade stepped up to the couple.

"Jasper? Where? How?"

"By the spot where *she* was," indicating Aurora. "Punctured in the jugular with this."

Chase and Aurora peered at the evidence bag Renegade held, containing a small Swiss army knife.

"It was discovered in her camera bag upon being searched." Ren turned to Aurora. "Is it yours?"

Aurora frowned. "It looks like mine, and I did have one in my bag. But I didn't kill anyone. I don't even know a Jasper." She had a déjà vu moment of being questioned by the Deadwood detectives. Maybe she was killing people and blanking it all out? She wasn't that kind of person, though. It just didn't make sense.

Ren turned to Chase. "As you probably know, Jasper was Cree Nation and they aren't very happy with the event being tainted by her. And now with this murder…" Ren let the sentence drop, knowing Chase would be very aware of the volatile issue at hand.

The threesome was interrupted when the small, heavy-muscled man called for their attention. "I'm Standing Bear, police of the Lakota. We'll handle it."

Ren turned around to face him. "I'm Ren. I'm a

detective in Texas and used to handling murder cases. My partner, Apple, is not able to move around much due to her delicate state, but she's wonderful at dealing with forensics. We're happy to offer our expertise and assistance."

Standing Bear nodded to Ren. "Thank you for the aid. Don't deal much with murderers."

"Glad to help." He handed the evidence bag over to Standing Bear. "The knife has blood on it and there is some blood at the bottom of the camera bag where the knife was discovered. I suggest you keep her under guard until we solve the crime."

"Just kill her now. You all waited and see what happened. Even if she didn't physically do it, she's brought evil among us. She's disrupted the peace we've had for centuries." Brandon burst into the center.

Unconsciously, Aurora shrunk behind Chase. She didn't know why Brandon seemed to hate her so, but his disposition frightened her.

"Back off, bro. Let the detective figure out what happened."

"Has the SD from her camera been destroyed yet?" Ren ignored Brandon's outburst.

"Yes. Almost immediately after she was discovered. But we haven't found the other one yet. There were only a couple of pictures on the one we did find inside her camera, but nothing useful," Standing Bear responded. He turned to her. "Where is it?"

She quietly reached into her pocket and took out one of the SD cards. She didn't mention the one still in her bra, though, as she'd forgotten about it in all the commotion.

"I'm going to bring the knife to Apple. She always has a fingerprinting kit with her. We'll also need Aurora's prints for comparison. I'll also have Apple take a look at the pictures on the card and see if there is anything we could use as evidence. We might even find a clue."

"I can take those and bring them to your partner." Standing Bear gathered the camera bag with gloved hands so as not to contaminate the evidence.

"Why are you all being so nice? She deserves to die for knowing about us; disrupting our rituals, bringing tragic catastrophe here." Brandon stepped closer to intimidate them in his persuasion.

Standing Bear turned to Brandon. "Settle down or leave. We'll handle this appropriately and without your interference." Giving his attention to Chase, "Bring her to the cave. I'll get her prints and interrogate her, then you."

"Yes, sir."

Chase led Aurora through the group, needing to push Brandon back. Aurora gasped for air as Chase led her to a set of structures put together, but she quickly recovered. It reminded Aurora of a sweat lodge, but thankfully it was dark and wasn't stifling with heat.

Standing Bear followed them both. "Chase, please wait outside. I would like to talk to her alone."

Chapter Eleven

Releasing Aurora, he gave her a longing look before he departed. Chase wanted to tell her so much more, but he couldn't. He believed in her, knew she couldn't kill anyone, and though he wanted to investigate himself, he knew he'd only be in the way.

He'd met Detectives Shaw and Shade centuries ago and knew they only recently entered the police force. He was aware of their reputation for fairness and efficiency and trusted them to not be persuaded by circumstantial evidence or negative rumors and assumptions. Something he himself found hard to do overall.

Trusting others outside of his band, his family, had never been easy for him. He lived through the treatment of the new settlers upon their world, taking their lands, giving them diseases, killing their food source, trying to commit cultural genocide, which included taking children away and putting them in boarding schools to eliminate all cultural customs and bonds.

Add to that the multitude of times he'd been personally burned, he found it hard to trust many people. He gave up a lot just to be free, frivolous and carefree. That was his style. Play. Have fun. No cares, no concerns, no entanglements, no staying around long enough anywhere or with anyone to give a damn. He refused to be hurt again. It's why he eventually moved out to his own parcel of land. Alone was better than having his heart torn into tiny shreds or be constantly reminded of it.

Then Aurora crashed into his life and he fell hard. No matter how he tried, he couldn't help but care about her. Her spirit, her fearlessness, her ferocity for life. He was smitten like some love-sick teenager. How she wormed her way into his very soul, he'd never know or even understand.

The soul wanted what or who it wanted, and he was powerless to stop the longing he had for her the moment he saw her making her way to the bull pens. Even then he longed to touch her, hold her, kiss her, claim her. He hated to let her go, but to protect her, he'd do anything. He'd been positive he'd never see her again, and it took all the strength he had to leave the warmth of her bed, and her luscious body, the following morning. But he should've known their story wasn't complete when he found her taking pictures of their event. God, he could've killed her for the danger she'd once again put herself in. And yet, there was a part of him absolutely thrilled to see her. He didn't break his oath by hunting her down. Instead, she came to him.

He scented her in the Sanctuary yesterday. Stared right at her and knew she'd seen him. He'd shifted into a hawk and watched her a bit longer before his duties called to him. He should've known she'd not be able to stay away. Due to the crowds of people, it took him a bit longer before he'd picked up her scent again, but he knew she was there the moment he did. Just where she didn't belong. Again.

His animal pranced in excitement, knowing she was near, and then in fear and anger at her being there. He didn't think he'd be able to help her unless he got her out before the others discovered her. He hadn't expected Brandon or the fierceness with which he attacked.

Unconsciously, Chase rubbed his chest, the only place not bandaged regardless of the scratches. He'd never known Brandon to be so antagonistic and he didn't understand why. He was also aware of Brandon's persuasive ability to sway the elders in sentencing Aurora to death.

Chase was sure they were going to condemn her, and the very thought made him sick. But he was flabbergasted beyond belief when Zonta told them Aurora carried his child. And he knew it was the truth.

The last time when they came, he floated out of his body. It was a legend he'd only heard about and never before experienced. He thought he'd imagined it. The idea was too incredulous at the time to have been thought of as anything other than fantasy with a touch of vertigo. He thought it was because it was the first time *ever* he'd been truly and whole-heartedly sated and that was what pure release felt like.

How many centuries had he been with women and never once experienced anything like it? He was pretty positive it was something others made up to entertain themselves during male bonding out on the range. He couldn't even remember the last time he'd even heard of such an event and therefore couldn't be blamed for not remembering such stories or believe them to be true.

Their souls merging meant they were to be together and bring a new life into the world. He was about to be a father. He had a mate. If only she would accept him.

Chase clenched his fist as he strode around the village. He had a bone to pick with Brandon. Never had he known his long-time friend to act in such a way. Ever since they were in Deadwood, Brandon had been acting with extreme prejudice. Normally, he was a compatriot spirit, but the last few days had Chase perplexed. He'd never expected Brandon to be so violent towards him, not after all these years.

Chase rubbed his chest again. Yeah, he needed to talk to Brandon. With a purposeful stride and focus, Chase headed into the circle to begin his search.

It took him a while to find Brandon coming away from the elder's circle. He looked none too happy, but then Chase wasn't thrilled with Brandon either.

"Brandon. Bro. Wait. We need to talk."

"I'm not going to change my mind, Chase. No matter what you think, Aurora is not good for you."

"What do you have against her? She has done nothing to you."

"No, but she's done something to you. You ain't been this enamored since Bianca, and I saw how that almost killed you. I ain't going to let it happen again."

"Bianca was different. She's a gold-digger. She used me in hopes of making Running Water jealous and get him to marry her so she could become the Chief's daughter-in-law. When I threatened those chances and she tried to kill me, I finally figured it out."

"But she had to go as far as stabbing you before

you figured it out. Even then you clung onto her as if she were in some play and would come back to you. I ain't never seen anyone as heartbroken as you, dude."

"It took a long while, but I did get over her."

"You sure 'bout that?"

"She came back about fifty years ago and told me she wanted me after all. I told her I wasn't interested."

Brandon's jaw dropped in shock. "Dude! I had no idea."

"I know. I let her save face by not publicly announcing her attempt. But I have no interest in her for that matter; I've not been interested in anyone since Bianca. Until now. Aurora is amazing and I wish you'd give her a chance."

Brandon shook his head. "I know you don't believe me, but there is something wrong with that woman. I don't trust her or you with her. You were warned by the elders, for fuck's sake, not to be with her. Why? Why care now when they ain't ever cared before? Can't you see the problem here? And now she's seen what we are, what you are. She needs to die."

"Even though she is carrying my child? Doesn't that mean anything to you?"

Brandon sighed, pinching his nose briefly. "Bro. I get it. But I'm not going to change my opinion. I'm sorry an innocent life will be destroyed in the meantime, but as far as I'm concerned, worse will happen if she lives. One innocent life is better than all of ours."

"She wouldn't do anything to harm us. She'd keep our secret."

"How do you know that?"

"I know. There's something about her from the moment I first saw her. An integrity. A deep sense of values, especially of what's right and wrong. She sympathized with our plight when I told her the truth about the Six Grandfathers Mountain. It angered her."

"Just because she sympathized doesn't make her safe. She'd probably turn right around and sell us out the first moment she could."

Chase's blood heated up beyond trying to reason with him and he slugged Brandon right in the face, knocking him onto the ground.

Brandon snarled up at Chase as he regained his feet. "Sorry you don't like to hear the truth, but you can't ignore it either."

Chase shook his head. "Man. I don't know what your problem is, but stay away from Aurora and the council. None of us need your input in deciding Aurora's and my future." He turned his back on Brandon, dismissing him as he did so.

Brandon snarled and tackled Chase from behind, knocking him on all fours while he remained on top of him.

Chase twisted about and the two began punching each other, their fists and bottled up anger meeting blow after blow.

The ruckus caused many others to form a circle around the two men, watching them pummel each other for several minutes. Kyle finally broke through the crowd and, once he realized who was fighting, he tried to pull Brandon off Chase. Raven also stepped in and held Chase back. Neither was an easy job as both men struggled against the ones holding them in order to continue fighting, but neither Kyle nor Raven would release their hold.

Finally Chase managed to shrug off Raven. "I'm good. I'm good."

Brandon calmed down enough for Kyle to usher him away from the group, and once they were gone, Chase stomped off in the opposite direction. He had hoped getting to talk to Brandon would settle things; instead the situation only seemed worse. He never in a million years would've thought Brandon would turn against him like that, but then he once never thought Bianca would either. Maybe he really was a very poor judge of character, and if that were the case, then maybe he was wrong about Aurora too. Maybe she couldn't be trusted. Regardless though, he wouldn't see her put to death while she was carrying his child. He wouldn't let an innocent suffer because of the deeds of his parents. And he still couldn't get over the fact that Aurora was also innocent. She just had to be. He couldn't really be wrong again. Could he?

Chapter Twelve

Ren and Standing Bear paced the small enclosure in opposing directions, perfectly choreographed so they didn't run into each other. Aurora thought it almost comical, if not for the dire situation.

"What time did you get here?" Ren rubbed the back of his neck.

"My answer isn't going to change no matter how many times you ask me."

"Don't be glib. Just answer the question," Standing Bear snarled at her.

Ren is the good cop and Standing Bear the bad cop. How cliché, Aurora thought, trying hard not to purse her lips at the idea. "About 5:30 this morning. I wanted to get situated before too many arrived and I'd be more noticeable."

"What did you do all day?"

"I set up my equipment and made sure I was pretty concealed before I took a small nap. The drums woke me up and I observed as well as took pictures." She'd already apologized more than a dozen times. She wasn't about to do it again. She'd realized it was a senseless attempt.

"When did you see Jasper?" Ren repeated the question as often as he had the others.

"I didn't see anyone in particular until Chase found me."

"We're getting nowhere," Standing Bear explained, exasperated.

"It's a process," Ren replied, though he had to admit they didn't seem to be getting anywhere with their questions. He turned back to Aurora. "Do we have all the pictures you took?"

"The SD was in the camera when I was discovered. And I already turned over another card as well."

"Do you know what makes me a great detective? I can tell when someone is not quite telling me everything. So, I ask you again, do we have all of the pictures you took while you were here?"

Aurora was about to deny it, but it wasn't worth it. Not when someone had died and she was being blamed for his murder. She reached into her bra and abashedly pulled out the small SD card, holding it out in her open palm. "This is the only other one I have. I swear to you."

"Holy shit," exclaimed Standing Bear, but couldn't grab it before Ren did.

"We need to see what's on here before we destroy it," Ren explained, tucking the card in his pocket.

"Why?"

"A possible clue."

"You expect her to film Jasper's murder as she was doing it?"

Ren snorted. "You assume she killed a man? A powerful shifter?"

Standing Bear peered closely at her and lowered his eyes in chagrin.

Aurora knew she wasn't a petite woman, but she'd seen a sampling of their strength and power. If Jasper was like the others, he wasn't an ordinary man to have over-powered him so easily, and she realized Ren understood that.

"It doesn't take a lot of strength to cut his carotid artery with a knife," Standing Bear stated matter of factly after he'd had a moment to think about it.

"True," Renegade agreed. "Still, she'd have had to have gotten pretty close to him brandishing the weapon. I would postulate she could've approached from behind, but again, I don't think Jasper would've let anyone sneak up on him. Especially someone he would've realized didn't belong here."

Standing Bear nodded. "You're good at this. I don't deal with murders often, if at all."

"Sadly, I do."

Kyle entered the area and handed Ren a note, threw Aurora a glance, before he hastily departed.

Ren read the note and sighed as he tossed it aside. "Apple states the knife was wiped and the only partial found was too smudged to be definitive."

"So, what do we do?" Standing Bear tilted his head towards Aurora.

She desperately wanted to remind them she was still in the room but decided remaining silent was the better option.

"Honestly, I'm not sure. I'd like to have Apple check out the SD cards and see what, if anything, is on it of use. I'd also like to go over Jasper's body again and see what, if anything, can be discerned from his remains."

Aurora couldn't stay quiet any longer. "I didn't do anything wrong other than take pictures and learn your secret. A secret no one in the world would believe. Hell, I saw it happen twice and still can't believe it. I'm not going to tell anyone. I'd be thrown into a mental institution if I did."

Standing Bear was about to say something that Ren was pretty positive wouldn't be appropriate. Instead, Ren put his hand on Standing Bear's shoulder. "Why don't you leave us alone for a couple of minutes?"

Standing Bear was about to refuse, but then turned and stomped out of the room. Once it was just the two of them, Ren sat opposite her. "Look, I know you're scared. There's a lot going on and your life hangs in the balance. I'll tell you this much. I don't think you did it. Killed Jasper, I mean. Which means someone else here did. After centuries of peace, it's hard to contemplate one of our own doing such a hideous thing. Which is why they're all anxious to make you the scapegoat.

"My wife is Feather. You met her earlier. When I met her again, a few years ago, it was because she was at the heart of a serial killer investigation. One of our kind, no less. She remembered how worried she was about being accused, and worse, the killer being after her, so I can comprehend how you must be feeling and how worried Chase must be."

"Worried?" Aurora was skeptical. "I've become an obligation to him. A nuisance. Nothing more."

"Is that what you truly think?"

"It's what I know. We'd put no promises on anything more than a fun night together."

Ren clenched his jaw. He didn't know Chase

beyond a cursory introduction when he and his band first arrived, but Ren was a detective. He read people pretty well, and Ren was sure Chase felt Aurora was more than an obligation or nuisance. He'd physically fought Brandon to protect her. Ren knew from personal experience that feeling of protection and helplessness Chase had to be feeling, but somehow Aurora didn't see it or thought it a farce. "Those of us chosen to have these special abilities bestowed upon us and our descendants have experienced a great deal of things during our lifetimes. Most of us find life a bit…repetitive…monotonous. It's the relationships we have that make life enjoyable and enriching."

Aurora tilted her head slightly. "Your point?"

"My point is, when we do feel something, it's intensified. It's more powerful than words can ever describe. It's all consuming. You may think Chase feels only obligation because you now carry his child, but I've seen him look at you. Watch you. He feels more than obligation.

"I'm not going to presume to know what you

feel for him or how he feels for you, I'm only stating that you need to talk to him and listen to him with an open mind." Ren stood and patted his pocket. "I'd best be headed over to Apple's and see what can be discerned, if anything, from your SD cards before we destroy them."

"Do you have to destroy all of the pictures? Surely there are some I could keep? Some that are not incriminating to what you all are or showing anything that might be sacred to you?"

Ren took a deep breath. "I'll see. I doubt it, but I'll see what you have and what the council thinks. That's the best I can do."

Aurora nodded. "I appreciate it."

Kyle burst into the room, pale and slightly out of breath. "Bianca! She was just found dead!"

Ren glanced briefly at Aurora, who gave him a blank stare in return. Giving a soft sigh, he turned back to Kyle. "Did anyone touch the body?"

"No. Shelby is guarding it with Chase until you come to take a look. Standing Bear sent me to get you and keep a watch on her."

Just then, a tall thin man walked in. He looked gaunt, almost too thin, and Aurora wondered how old this man was, for he already looked like he was eighty. "I'm to sit with her until you've finished with Bianca. Standing Bear wants you to help him with the body, Kyle."

Ren nodded but stopped as he passed by the older man, resting his hand on his shoulder. "I'm very sorry for your loss, Shel."

The older man nodded in return but growled low and almost animalistic. "Find the bitch or bastard that did this to my precious."

"I will. I promise you that much," Ren firmly stated as he ducked out with a reluctant Kyle following on his heels.

Aurora assumed this was the same Shelby who found the poor unfortunate woman and was with Chase originally. Then something dawned on her, a realization that might actually help her and her protests of innocence. There was no way she could've killed Bianca since she'd been under careful watch.

She stood, but swifter than she could believe possible for such an aged person, Shelby was in front of her.

"Sit down and don't move or you'll wish you hadn't," he snarled threateningly.

"Sorry." She held her hands up defensively as she slowly sat back down, folding her hands in her lap and waiting for the others to return.

Chapter Thirteen

Standing Bear and Chase had moved the onlookers away by the time Ren arrived, and he was grateful to not have such a large crowd standing about. The drums had died down, the dancing stopped. Groups of people stood amongst their own band whispering and gesturing. The sacred mood of celebration had been broken several times now, between discovering the outsider, to finding first Jasper, and now Bianca both ruthlessly murdered and no one seeing a thing.

Ren understood how upset everyone was and the helpless concern others felt that a murderer walked among them. After centuries of peaceful gatherings and maintaining the rules of conduct between them for peace, regardless of any conflicts they might otherwise have, only to have it destroyed in just a few hours, multiple times, seemed incomprehensible.

Bending over, Ren examined the body. There were no visible marks, other than bruises on her body, and her neck lay at an odd angle, obviously broken. He could hear the whispers of the others who insisted the female outsider was to blame, but they were not detectives, unlike him. Ren knew Aurora was a frail human who would never have the ability to sneak up on Jasper, much less catch him off guard enough to plunge a knife into his carotid artery. But with Bianca, there was no possibility of Aurora committing the murder. Strangulation and broken necks were almost always done by men, for women didn't have the strength to succeed in such strenuous methods. Against a shifter, it would be nigh on impossible for a human to have the strength to commit the murder.

Something else was going on here, and it bothered Ren that he couldn't quite put his finger on it. Admittedly, he was slightly out of his comfort zone. He was used to the hustle and bustle of San Antonio, Texas. He knew the dank areas of the Riverwalk and the secret places of the missions, but this was unknown territory, and as such, he just couldn't fathom exactly what was occurring.

Slipping into Apple's tipi after she called for

him to enter, he moved over to her cot and knelt beside her. Apple Shade has been his police partner for a couple of decades, and as of the last couple of years they were also in-laws. While Ren had married Feather, Apple had married Feather's brother, Raine, and both couples were expecting their first child due only weeks apart. However, Apple was having a slightly harder time with her pregnancy, and the journey to South Dakota had been far more taxing than any thought imaginable. Had any of them any inkling, they would've insisted she refrain from the voyage despite the insistence of their band for them to go. Ren could only contemplate that the Comanche and Kiowa elders knew their expertise would desperately be needed here. Their powers of foreseeing the future were as pronounced as Zonta's of the Sioux.

"What goodies did you bring me this time?" Apple glowed with the promise of motherhood, and even Ren had to admit he was glad to see Apple in such a state. Of course, she was nowhere near the perfection of the woman he had loved for a couple of hundred years, and finally won, but Apple was important to him, both as a partner and as a friend who was also an in-law.

"Nothing much, physically. But I need your mind, Apple. Something is going on and I just can't quite put it together. We've always worked best discussing the case, and this one has a multitude of twists and surprises as any we've come across since the case that brought us Raine and Feather."

Apple frowned and sat up, moving the pillows to help support her back. "Okay. Tell me everything you know."

"You know some of it already. Chase has a human girl he got pregnant and she happened to spy on the group's dancing, taking some pictures." He shifted slightly to reach in his pocket and pull out the two SD cards and handed them to her. "The first one from the camera barely had any pictures on it, so we knew that there had to be more. She just produced the last one recently. Maybe there will be something on there that will help with the case. You may or may not have heard, but we have a second murder. A woman named Bianca, who I'm told was once involved with Chase. Aurora *could've* known about Bianca, maybe even been jealous, or Bianca could've been jealous over Aurora and the fact that Aurora now carries Chase's child, but when? Would Bianca have had time to confront Aurora? Or for that matter, for Aurora to have killed her? There wouldn't have been any reason for Bianca to be jealous of Aurora until after Aurora was discovered and we learned that Aurora was carrying Chase's child. Since then, Aurora has been in our custody the entire time, making it impossible for her to have killed Bianca after being discovered.

"Aurora states once she got into her observation spot, she'd fallen asleep until the drums woke her and then she didn't move, too busy taking pictures."

"How long has Bianca been dead for? Do we have any idea?"

"Not exactly. One of her tribesmen stated the last time they saw her was late afternoon, just before we started the dances. And…before we knew about Aurora being here. But here's another thing. Aurora is human. Bianca was strangled."

"Then Aurora is innocent. It's virtually impossible for a human to strangle one of our kind, male or female. That means it would more likely be a shifter. At this point, Chase seems like he'd be the logical choice. He'd have had the opportunity and a possible motive. You said they were not together any longer. She could've been jealous that Chase didn't want her. He could've wanted to make sure she didn't interfere with him if he chose to pursue Aurora." Apple tapped her hand against her thigh as she thought. "But what do any of them have to do with the Cree, Jasper?"

"That's only one of the things perplexing. If Aurora killed Jasper, as many are trying to convince us of, why? She didn't know him, that anyone is aware of. And yet, hitting his carotid artery is an up-close-and-personal action. If she struck him from behind, he must have been sure she wasn't a threat to not even turn around. If she approached him from the front, he let her get awfully close for someone he didn't know. And hitting that kind of artery would've made quite a mess with the arterial spray, yet Aurora is pristine from blood on her."

"Do we have a time of death for Jasper? Approximately?"

"It's estimated around the same time Chase and Brandon got into the brawl over Aurora. Maybe shortly thereafter. Either way, Aurora was hiding until Chase found her, and then she's not been left alone since. So how could she have murdered Jasper, much less Bianca?"

Apple shook her head as she contemplated everything. "She couldn't. Not unless she were one of us, and even then, she'd be hard pressed. Nothing like a couple of hundred people around as possible witnesses."

"I know. No one can be that bold to kill someone in almost plain sight."

They both sat in silence going over everything until finally Ren stood. "I'll check back with you in a bit. In the meantime, take a look at those pictures and see if you see anything. Since I highly doubt she is the killer, she might have caught who did with her candid shots."

"If I find anything, I'll send for you immediately."

Chapter Fourteen

Chase wrung his hands. If Bianca wasn't already dead, he was pretty sure he'd strangle her. Still a part of him ached over Bianca. Unconsciously, his hand rubbed his cheek where she'd slapped him over two centuries ago, remember that event. Even today he recalled every word of her betrayal.

"Marry you?" Bianca spat in his face. "You're nothing to me. I only tolerated your company to make Running Water notice me. He's in line to be chief and as his wife, I'll be in power to be listened to."

Chase used his arm to wipe the spit away. She'd used him so callously and he never knew. Never suspected. He was a great hunter, a desirable mate, but he wasn't the chief's son and he couldn't give her the prestige she so desperately desired. He reached for her and she slugged him in the face. "Stay away from me." She stormed out of his tipi and left him in shock.

Worse, she told him all of this after she'd made

love to him, going down on him. It had been such an intimate thing he couldn't ever let another woman go down on him again. Not ever. Not even Aurora. It'd hurt too much. Bianca devastated him so much he remained celibate for decades.

Brandon had stood by his side the entire time, supported him, convinced him to at least get his urges taken care of. Bianca was also why Chase had been burned so badly, he'd had no desire for women of his own kind.

Then one hundred and fifty years later, after Bianca tore his beating heart out of his chest, Bianca sought him out.

"I want you." Bianca almost begged him about fifty years ago, after Running Water used then discarded her to marry someone else.

"Well, I don't want you." Chase laughed at her. Did she really think he'd forget the last hundred and fifty years when she spurned him to be with Running Water? "I was never willing to be your second choice."

He'd turned his back on her, underestimating

her ferocity. She stabbed him in the shoulder and before she could strike again, Brandon tackled her knocking the knife out of her hand.

But now Aurora didn't want him either, yet despite that, Aurora was being blamed for Bianca's death as well as Jasper's and he knew it was Brandon who was spreading the lies. He still couldn't figure out why Brandon was so antagonistic against Aurora. She'd never been anything but nice to his friend and yet, Brandon's attitude continued to become more belligerent with each passing moment.

He needed to find Brandon again and have it out with him about Aurora. Killing her wouldn't help find the real killer, nor would it save their long standing friendship. Nothing made sense to Chase, but then, he was still reeling from the news that Aurora carried his child. What if he'd just let her go as they had both planned. She might've had an abortion or decided to raise the child alone, not knowing what his offspring would be capable of. Would she have even bothered to try and find him in order to tell him of her situation? Somehow, he didn't think so. From what he had learned of her, he was sure she wouldn't have told him in case he might think she was burdening him with a child that might not have even been his. But he knew better. He knew she couldn't have slept around or that the child would be someone else's. Everything, like now, would've slipped into place and he wouldn't be able to deny his child.

Yet, the blessed news of him becoming a father was dampened by so many exigent circumstances. It was her pregnancy which stayed her immediate execution for learning their secrets. However, if she is convicted of Jasper's and Bianca's deaths, they might overlook the fact of her condition and end her life or hold her prisoner until she gave birth and then put her to death. Chase was sure he wouldn't be able to bear such an outcome. Why did she have to be so damned curious? Hadn't she ever heard curiosity killed the cat? He'd almost rather not know she was pregnant if it would've avoided all of this.

Still, he knew, deep inside, Aurora didn't murder Jasper and Bianca. So, the question was, who did? He had to find Brandon. Maybe, just maybe, Brandon would put aside his animosity and help him uncover the truth. If only, he could find him. Sure, he should just let Brandon go, but Brandon had stood by him for so many years, for so many things, he was sure he could work it out with him about Aurora, even after their last brawl.

Chase headed towards Brandon's tipi, then the circle but he couldn't find Brandon anywhere. Unsure where to go next he met up with Ren and Standing Bear headed back to the cave.

"Did you find anything yet to prove her innocence?" Chase asked.

Ren shook his head. "Apple is checking over Aurora's photos but nothing yet. So far, if Brandon hadn't shifted in front of her, I don't think she'd have known about our special attributes."

"There still would've been a problem with her pregnancy. Had you not learned of this, she'd be freaking out when the child reached puberty and his or her gifts started to manifest." Standing Bear crossed his arms over his massive chest.

"I do have some bad news though." Ren shifted his stance to one side, knowing Chase wouldn't like what he'd discovered, and Standing Bear would be upset for not being involved.

"What?" Chase held his breath.

"I had Apple contact the Deadwood Police since I'd heard that's where she'd been staying and they have two death investigations going on. One, was a woman who was stabbed to death by the PBR grounds and the other was a woman found strangled in the Franklin. The same hotel Aurora is at and was only a couple of doors away. The detectives have photos of Aurora in the hallway by the woman's room around the same time as the woman was killed. It also appears Aurora knew the woman." Ren announced somberly. "As for the other woman who was stabbed, the weapon was a small pocket switchblade like the one that killed Jasper. The detectives didn't go into too much detail of the wounds, but the killing blow was her throat being sliced open."

Chase frowned. "I remember the police being there when I dropped her off. Surely, they can't believe Aurora had anything to do with that? Who was the woman?"

Ren pulled out his notebook from his back jeans pocket. "An Allison Harper from Bismarck, North Dakota. The detectives on the case, Detective Collins and Hansley told Aurora not to leave town. They actually have more questions for her but Apple told them we were looking into two deaths here and reservation land, aka government land took precedence. I'm to keep them informed on any and all progress with the case and any indications that the cases overlap.

"A bit of a coincidence there, don't you think?" Standing Bear tapped his foot unconsciously.

"Maybe but there are too many questions. Like how could a human female surprise Jasper enough to stab him. And how could she have gotten close to Bianca when she was with us the whole time? My time as a detective I've learned that women don't strangle because they rarely have the strength to break the hyoid. I don't see Aurora being able to do the crimes here and if she didn't do the ones here, I highly doubt she did the ones in Deadwood. The question is who was in both places that could?"

Standing Bear nodded. "I know Yellow Bear had Kyle follow her for a while. He might have seen something?"

"We might want to talk to Kyle, though if he had seen something, I'm sure he would've reported it. We might also wish to talk to Brandon and you, as well, Chase as both of you were in town for the PBR event.

"Of course. I understand, although if I knew anything, I would've mentioned it before."

"But you didn't know about these cases Deadwood PD is working on which involve Aurora."

Chase acquiesced. "Agreed. I didn't." He frowned. Ren was right. There were way too many coincidences for his peace of mind.

Chapter Fifteen

Aurora leaned back against the wall. She was suddenly exhausted and there wasn't anything she could do until the cops did their investigation. Hopefully, they were smart enough to figure out what she already had. She couldn't have killed Bianca because she wasn't alone at any time since Chase found her hiding.

Aware that Shelby found Bianca and was somehow related to her, she remained still and silent out of respect for the older man who just lost someone obviously dear to him.

Despite the warmth of the day, the setting sun was making the cave cooler. She was therefore slightly surprised when Shelby approached her to hand her a blanket. She looked up at his reddened eyes, grateful for his thoughtfulness during his own grief. "Thank you."

"Did you do it?" His voice was raspy and choked up from his grief.

She shook her head. "No. I've been with someone the entire time."

"Not before you were discovered."

"True. But I hadn't moved from my spot until I was found. I didn't know Bianca. Or Jasper, or anyone else here. I am not a violent person and I am not a killer."

He nodded and sat back down away from her but watching.

"Was she your wife?"

He barked once at that. "No. She was my daughter, and she was promised to Chase. Or so she told me, but I have a feeling Chase didn't feel the same way about her and was one of the reasons why he petitioned to join the PBR. Honestly, she'd had her chance to be with him centuries ago. I didn't know her as Bianca. Many were given names when they were forced into boarding schools in order to give up their culture. To me, she was Shappa. It means Red Thunder."

"I'm sorry. I didn't know. We weren't together long enough to talk about each other's past relationships."

Again he nodded, and she didn't know what

else to say. Wrapping the blanket around her shoulders, she leaned back against the stone and soon found her eyes very heavy, shutting them.

Shelby watched her. He felt a presence behind him, but didn't bother to look up, assuming it was Chase, Ren or Standing Bear. He didn't want to take his eyes off of Aurora, still unsure if she was the culprit or not. It surprised him when her eyes popped open, but seemed to be staring at nothing. A wispy, eerie voice came from her lips, sending chills down his body.

"Careful. He's here."

Shelby turned around quickly, just as a knife barely missed his throat. But the wielder of the weapon was swift and pounced on Shelby in a heartbeat, managing to plunge the blade into the old man's jugular, the spray of blood splattering the walls and Aurora. Immediately, the younger man moved towards her and grabbed her by the throat, pulling her into a standing position. Aurora reached out, pounding her fists against him as he continued to lift her into the air. Her legs were swinging as she kicked him, but he withstood all of her attacks, seemingly unfazed.

"You won't win this time," Aurora squeaked out in a raspy, eerie voice.

"It won't matter. You're a slut. A whore. You need to die. You will die, and by my hand."

"You have no power over me. You never did. That's why you hate me so much."

"I have more than you realize." He tilted his head before he dropped her unceremoniously to the ground. "We'll meet again to finish this. Never fear." He swiftly departed, his words rebounding about the cave.

Moments later, Ren, Chase and Standing Bear entered the cave only to discover the horrific sight that awaited them. Aurora stood over Shelby's body, the bloody knife at her feet, staring frightened as she saw the others enter. "I didn't do it. I swear."

Ren held Standing Bear back with a light hand on his bicep before he stepped forward and squatted beside Shelby, checking for a pulse, then shaking his head slightly to indicate his passing. "I suggest you inform the elders, Standing Bear, while I deal with Ms. Taylor."

A low, menacing growl came from Standing Bear, who hesitated before he spun on his heel and stomped out of the cave.

Chase moved to Aurora. Seeing her shiver uncontrollably, he pulled her into his arms for warmth and comfort. He looked around for something else to help warm her, knowing it was more likely shock than cold that had her shaking so violently, but the blanket at her feet was soaked in blood and there wasn't another one around.

Ren pulled off his jacket and handed it to Chase to wrap Aurora in, ushering them both away from Shelby's corpse. "Wanna tell us what happened?"

Ren tried to be impartial, but even this didn't appear to bode well for Aurora, and his belief that she was innocent of the other two murders now came into question. Maybe he was dealing with a cold-blooded psychopath.

"I… I don't know. I know that sounds strange, because I was here the entire time, but I really don't know."

Chase pulled her into his arms and she didn't refuse him this time. "It's okay, Aurora. You're probably in shock. Just take a couple of deep breaths and focus. Tell us what you remember," he cooed softly against her ear, trying to calm her trembling body.

Ren was grateful for Chase's words. Maybe he'd be able to get some truth from her.

She followed Chase's instructions, and after a moment, she tried again. "Shelby gave me his blanket to keep warm against the dampness of the ground and walls. I remember getting very sleepy as a result, and then…I guess I fell asleep. I heard a loud thump and that woke me. When I looked around for the sound, Shelby was on the ground at my feet, and then you guys came into the room. I'm sorry, I wish I knew more."

"That's the lamest thing I ever heard in my life." Brandon sauntered into the room and looked down at Shelby before returning his gaze to Chase. "She needs to be executed. She's already killed three people here and god knows how many back in Deadwood."

"Deadwood? What do you mean? What are you talking about?" Ren pulled out his notebook to take some notes. He was aware of the murders in Deadwood but was unsure how Brandon knew about them.

"I remember when we were at the PBR, there was some talk of a couple of women killed during the week of the event. I never gave it much thought until now, but one of the women was found in her room at the Franklin, and if I remember correctly, Chase, that is where Aurora is staying."

Chase grimly nodded his confirmation. "I remember seeing the cops around one of the times I brought her back to the hotel. They were on the floor she was staying on. But that has to be a coincidence. Aurora couldn't have killed those women. Right?" Although Chase had just mentioned as much to Ren and Standing Bear outside, he assumed if Ren was playing ignorant, then he should do the same.

Even Chase appeared uncertain of her innocence, and Aurora was disappointed that even he thought she might be a vicious killer. "I would never hurt anyone. Why would I? I have no motive. I didn't know the woman or women whose lives were taken." Her voice rose with each proclamation. "Just as I didn't know those who were killed here." She took a breath slowly, to try and sound more logical than she was feeling. "Look. I'm sorry for your losses, but honestly, I didn't do it. I don't know who did, which is awful, I know, since Shelby was obviously... That he was... That he...died...in front of me while I was asleep. I didn't know I could sleep that soundly, but I honestly didn't hear anything."

Ren jotted down a couple of notes, then flipped his notebook closed. "I'll have Standing Bear confirm with the Deadwood PD about the other, possibly similar deaths. Chase, take her back to your tipi and stay with her until we see what's going on. I need to talk with Standing Bear first, then check with Apple to see if Aurora's pictures will help prove her innocence." He gave a solemn look to Aurora and shook his head slightly. She was in a world of trouble and she couldn't even comprehend it all.

Although Shelby's death made him pause in his belief of her innocence, Renegade was sure of one thing—she was innocent until he could prove otherwise. It was only when Ren saw a glint of steel did his reverie break to a split-second action. He virtually jumped on Brandon, who pulled out a blade and was about to attack Aurora, tackling him to the ground. He grabbed Brandon's knife-wielding fist, banging it into the earth to get him to loosen his grip and drop it. A solid punch or two to Brandon's face finally caused him to release it, just as Chase was herding Aurora out of the cave and towards his tent.

"What the hell do you think you're doing?" Ren snarled as he pushed the knife away, letting Brandon settle back down.

"I was going to scalp her. I'm tired of waiting for permission to kill the bitch when she so obviously is killing our kind. She needs to die, and preferably at my hand. I want her dead, and I'm ready to do it myself."

Ren sighed, stood and helped Brandon up. "I get it. You're protecting your friend, your band. This whole reunion is screwed, blued and tattooed, but attacking Aurora now is a bit premature. Plus you are putting your friendship in danger. She is, after all, pregnant with Chase's child. Even if she is guilty, the child is innocent and won't be unduly sacrificed."

Brandon breathed deeply, still scowling as he rubbed his jaw. "You're right. He is my friend and I'll protect him with my dying breath, even if it's from women who just want something from him. I don't trust her. I never have, and I don't understand what he sees in her. She's been nothing but trouble from the moment he first laid eyes on her. She has brought our rituals, our event, nothing but condemnation and vexation since she entered his life. Our elders warned him against her and yet she still managed to disrupt our ceremonies and bring ruin to our people. With the death of Jasper, we are barely avoiding a war with the Cree. And the death of Bianca and now Shelby? We'll be lucky to survive any of this intact. All of these complications she's involved in will do nothing for the hundreds of years of peace and tranquility we've held during that time. She is the harbinger of evil, and despite any innocence she has conceived, it's not worth letting her live."

"I understand your position, but you're wrong and you'd be taking not one but two innocent lives. Aurora's and her child's. I know this is hard for you to believe at this moment, but I can guarantee you she did not kill Jasper or Bianca. As such, I don't believe she killed Shelby either, but the latter one is more difficult to prove at this moment. Give me a chance. If you don't trust me, trust in Chase and your elders. Let me find who is really causing these problems and get the right person to justice."

Brandon snarled, but then just frowned. "Fine. You have until tomorrow morning before I push for her death again. Find whoever is the real culprit or stand aside while I insist on her scalp."

Ren didn't respond at first. That really wasn't much time, but truth was, if they didn't find who the real murderer was by then, they might never do so. "Agreed. Till tomorrow morning."

Chapter Sixteen

Chase sat next to Aurora after placing another blanket around her shoulders to help keep her warm. He refused to leave her side. Someone had killed Shelby in front of her and then tried to murder her as well. She was in too much shock to remember much of what occurred and that concerned him. Whoever it was got close and personal in order to wrap their hands around her neck, which was now showing a slight imprint of discoloration he knew by morning would be full, outright bruises. He'd brought her back to his tipi, but neither spoke.

Once inside, he started to hand her a bottle of whiskey, but then pulled it back and boiled water for tea. He'd almost forgotten her pregnancy over the horrific events of the past few hours. Once the water was boiled, he made her some tea and handed her the clay mug. Shakily, she took it, giving him a brief grateful smile, then took a long swig of the liquid, coughing as it burned its way down her throat and into her belly. She didn't wait until the heat died down any. As soon as her coughing subsided, she pressed her lips against the mug, tilting it again and letting the dark liquid warm her insides further.

"I'm sorry. I never meant for any of this to happen. I just wanted to see…" She stopped. She'd said all of this before and repeating it wasn't going to change anything.

"I know. I just wish you'd remember who killed Shelby and tried to kill you. But even Standing Bear can't argue with the bruises beginning to appear on your neck. Whoever it was, Shelby trusted enough that he was caught unawares."

"But why? To get at me? I haven't done anything to warrant such treatment."

"To some…"

"Like Brandon?"

Chase pressed his lips together before responding. "Yes. Like Brandon. To some, who go by the old ways where all non-Natives are dangerous, the sentence is death to those who learn our secret and there are no exceptions. To them, you're an abomination who continues to live among us and therefore bring bad luck to all of us here."

"So, like a superstitious black cat crossing your path or a ladder for you all to walk under?"

Chase snorted. "Yeah. Something like that. I've overheard some of our band say that, because you're still here, others died to appease the Great Father. If it was just our band, most likely even Zonta wouldn't be able to protect you. But the Ojibwa, especially Hope and Raven, are a perfect example trying to change the elder's opinions that a non-Native can exist within our band."

"I don't want to co-exist. I'm not going to marry you and move to South Dakota just because I'm pregnant with your child."

"At least you've come to terms with being pregnant." Chase sighed. Nothing like being so dismissed by a woman he cared for. It must be what Bianca had felt when he refused her attentions. He wished he could've apologized to her, but her death was a sudden surprise to them all. He genuinely knew Bianca had treated him worse and he wasn't about to ever take her back, but he could understand a part of what she might have felt with his rejection of her. It was the same devastation he'd felt when Bianca dismissed him hundreds of years ago, and the way he was feeling now with Aurora treating him the same way. "You don't have to marry me. I won't continue to ask or beg for you to accept me as your husband. But you do carry my child, and as such, that does afford you certain…privileges. Like living."

Aurora had been holding the cup, using the heat from her tea to help warm her hands and inhaling the steam, but she'd set it down to the side and moved towards him slightly, taking his hands in hers. "Look. Everything is just moving way too fast. I am still trying to mentally accept what you truly are. What you all are. Then, I also have to deal with the fact some woman of your tribe tells me I'm pregnant with your child when we only had sex just a couple of days ago. Granted, it was beyond-my-wildest-dreams kind of sex, but in just two days,

I'm pregnant? It's unbelievable. To top it all off, not only your band wants me dead, but someone is going out of their way to try and accomplish it. Now let's just throw in this proposal that you most likely wouldn't have made until you found out I was pregnant with a child I'm still not one hundred percent sure I'm carrying. It's far too much. I can't... How can I marry you when you're only asking because you feel it's a duty? No. I won't marry you. Not now. Maybe not ever."

Chase stared down at her as he kept his face as stoic as possible, though the emotions were raging inside of him as she made her little speech. He couldn't blame her one iota. Everything she said was true, and when one wasn't accustomed to his unique world, things had to appear preposterous. "I didn't make the proposal because you are with my child, and I didn't make it solely to save your life. I admit those are the reasons that propelled me to make such a request of you, but I left you because I couldn't bear to leave you if I'd stayed for more than I did."

Chase dropped her hands and pulled her by the shoulders closer to him. "I admit that what I am feeling may or may not be love or infatuation. I've not let many get that close to really find out, but Aurora, you touched something deep inside of me the moment you climbed the bull pens. I still don't know what it is, but I am willing to spend my life with you to find out. Please. Give me a chance. Give *us* a chance."

She hesitated for several heartbeats, her own breath catching in her throat at the way he looked at her and made her feel. It was all she could manage to get out, an almost inaudible, "No."

He dropped his hands and stepped back, almost growling. He had nothing more to say, nothing more he *could* say. Without a word, he left the enclosure and stood outside, letting the cool air calm his heated veins.

Aurora watched him head out before she picked up the mug again, staring into the leafy brew. The more she stared into the mug, the more the mug faded away and fields of green came into her view with Chase laughing as two children ran around him, blowing bubbles while he cradled a third in his arms.

She'd had that vision once before, but this time it seemed stronger, almost realistic. Then, the scene changed as the open field became a graveyard while she watched a wooden coffin being lowered into the ground. The feeling of despair and sadness overwhelmed her. She didn't understand it, as this part of her vision seemed as if it were something from the past and not the future. She didn't notice the tears streaming softly down her cheeks. It wasn't until the mug fell to the ground, the clattering thud sounding, that her reverie was finally broken. She wiped her cheeks with the back of her hand. "Well, that's new."

Chapter Seventeen

Raine stood to let Ren in their tipi. Apple was propped up with lots of pillows, the laptop computer on her bent knees. Since his own wife, Feather, was also pregnant, he was well aware that odd positions were the only way the women could get comfortable. Raine returned to his wife and pulled a leg forward so he could rub her foot.

"Anything?" Ren moved to peer over her shoulder at the computer screen but was unsuccessful and had to wait beside her patiently while Apple scrolled through the pictures from the SD card.

"I've been going through the pictures and so far nothing unusual, but there are about a dozen I have yet to inspect. I'm just having a hard time getting comfortable. My back is killing me and my ankles are swollen like watermelons."

"Feather has only been fairing a bit better. Sadly, this case doesn't allow me time to be with her, like Raine. And I only have until the morning or Aurora is going to be put on trial by the elders that she has little chance of winning, judging from many of the people from other bands who are becoming more and more restless with each new death discovered. And the Cree are ready to go to war if the Sioux don't kill Aurora themselves. I need something, anything to prevent her death and thereby the death of her unborn child."

"So far, there isn't anything here. She's a wonderful photographer, but there's nothing…" Apple stopped all of a sudden, her brow furrowing as she looked at a picture.

"What? Did you find something?" Ren stood, anxious for anything Apple might've discovered.

"I'm not sure. This is awfully…strange. Look at this." She turned the screen around to let Ren see for himself.

At first, he didn't notice anything out of the ordinary. "What am I looking at?"

"Here." She pointed to the upper right hand of the screen. In the background was Jasper, standing with his arms folded over his chest. Next to him and slightly behind him, another figure was standing, but with an eerie glow around his body.

"What is that? Who is that? Is the sun reflecting off of him or something?" Ren asked, puzzled.

"Wait." Apple pulled the screen back for one moment to advance the picture and turned the computer to face Ren once again.

This time Ren could see the aura around the person more distinctly and it sent chills down Ren's spine. The ghostly figure of a white man appeared to take over the being it was encompassing, and the figure was dressed in garb from the 1800s. The body of the person who it was enshrouding was obscured by the ghostly countenance.

Apple took the computer back once more to push the next button and returned it to Ren. This time the ghostly figure seemed to know his face was being photographed, for he seemed to sneer in the camera's direction while the body was walking away.

"Could this be a trick shot of one picture taken over the other?" Ren rubbed his eyes, then pushed the buttons between the photos to peer at them more closely.

"I thought that too, but everything else is identical to the background. No overlapping. No other area showing a double exposure. I fear someone is possessed, and that the possessor is our actual culprit for all these crimes."

"I think you're right. Although it's a relief to have Aurora vindicated, I'm not sure what to do about a ghost possessing one of our own." Ren pulled the computer away from Apple altogether. "I'll need to show this to the elders. Hopefully they will know what to do in order to figure out who might be possessed and how to rid him of his unwanted guest."

"For some reason, this ghost, as you say, seems to have a grudge against Aurora. I'd make sure she is never alone. Something tells me this isn't over yet."

Ren frowned. "I fear you are correct, but I also think you and Feather could also be in danger. Bianca and Shelby were associated with Chase. And we are all associated with Aurora. If, in fact, this ghost is going after her, he may find substitutes in the interim with you or Feather." Ren turned slightly to face Raine. "If you don't mind, I'm going to send Feather here as well. Raine? I trust you to keep both our women safe until this is all resolved."

Raine placed Apple's foot onto the bedding and stood. "Of course. I'll protect both my sister and my wife with my very life. Get Feather and bring her here and I'll watch over them both."

Chapter Eighteen

Aurora bent over to pick up the fallen mug when she was pushed from behind, a hard body on top of her. She struggled and screamed. In moments, the weight was off her, so she quickly scrambled back until she'd hit the hide wall, seeing a slit not too far from where she currently was.

She turned back to the scene in front of her. She could see the behind of Chase rolling around with someone, but it wasn't until a glint of silver caught her eye that she became even more fearful. Only this time for Chase. The few places he hit with the blade were mostly parts of Chase that were already bandaged from Brandon's earlier attack.

"Help! Help!" Aurora jumped to her feet and dashed through the opening in the tipi.

Raven, Stone, Ren and others came rushing over, pushing her out of the way as two men, one being Chase, rolled outside in an embittered struggle.

*   *   *   *

Making sure Feather was safe and secure in Raine and Apple's tipi, Renegade headed to the elders' tents with the laptop and SD card of the pictures Aurora had taken. Although he had proof in his hands by way of pictures that Aurora was innocent of the deaths, Ren knew not all the pieces fit perfectly together.

Ren noticed Standing Bear next to the Ojibwa named Raven and his wife, Hope, as he neared the elders' circle. He quickened his pace and joined the threesome.

Standing Bear waited only long enough for Ren to be within hearing range and close enough he wouldn't have to make their business known to everyone around them. "Raven and Hope were just trying to convince me to speak on behalf of Ms. Taylor since their band accepted Hope, who is also human."

"I've got proof that Aurora didn't do those murders and there is something else going on here. I need to speak with the elders." Ren lifted up the laptop to make his point.

"Mind if I tag along? You've got me curious now," Raven asked after Hope poked him on his side, although he tried to pretend she didn't. He slipped his arm around her waist and kissed her temple, knowing she wouldn't be able to be in front of the traditionalistic elders at this time.

"Sure." Standing Bear headed toward the circle of elders, with Raven and Ren on either side of him, respectively.

Zonta waved around to the others. "Show us." She seemed to know what they were there for.

Ren squatted for balance in order to open up the computer and hand it over, showing the picture of the ethereal person surrounding a male figure. He waited for the questions to begin, as did the others.

"He's not the only one…infected," Zonta calmly stated.

"What do you mean?" Standing Bear was puzzled by such a statement. He'd gotten a glimpse of the pictures before Ren passed the computer over to the elders.

"Do you know who it is? How to get rid of it?"

"To get rid of it is easier than who it is. Maybe Aurora could tell us that, or maybe one of the others."

"She knows?"

"I've a sense a part of her knows the history of this person, but it's something she only learned recently. Humanly."

"Will you punish her for any of this?" Raven lowered his head respectively.

Mato shook his head. "No. We won't punish those who have come here influenced by others, otherwise we would be no better than those who did the influencing."

Mahkah handed the laptop back to Ren. "We will need to talk with Aurora."

Zonta raised her hand to gain attention. "Also Chase and Brandon, for they are also an essential part of what might yet to be divulged. Keep the pictures near, but they may be of use yet."

Ren put the computer next to Zonta and, with the other two men, left to retrieve the three needed for the elders' requested audience.

But as Ren neared Chase's makeshift abode, a commotion caused him to run the rest of the way.

*   *   *   *

Chase kept dodging the swinging blade, and everyone was trying to get close enough to separate the two men. No one was paying attention to Aurora, who suddenly went all glassy eyed.

At least until she pushed them aside. "Pierre Hills. You have no power here." She stretched out her hand and the knife that Kyle had been welding flew out of his hand and into hers.

Everyone looked up, astonished. Kyle pushed Chase away, giving him a side kick to his ribs as he did so. "So. You decided to come out and play after all?"

Aurora laughed, but it wasn't her that was amused, it was the being inside of her. "I couldn't stop you from killing Allison or Jeanette. Or those whom you took from here. But here is where you made your mistakes, Pierre."

"Mistakes? Lily-Anne, I've only succeeded here more than anywhere else."

The inhabited bodies of Aurora and Kyle seemed to pay no attention to those gathered around them. Ren shook his head and whispered for everyone to stay back. This needed to be played out between Pierre, who appeared to be in Kyle, and Lily-Anne, who was in Aurora.

Again, Lily-Anne laughed. "Your time has come."

"How so?" Kyle's eyes darkened with Pierre inside.

"Jeanette. Allison. Jasper. Bianca. Shelby. These I call as your last victims. I also call on the others you have murdered over the last century. Jacob. Maggie. Sarah. Jasmine. Reuben. Della. Daphne. Angela. Irene. Nathaniel. Stephanie. Theresa. Margaret. Phyllis. Isaac. Come. Come."

For the first time, Pierre looked around frightened. When nothing seemed to happen, he chuckled furtively.

Lily-Anne lifted her arms and seemed to step

out of Aurora's body, which crumpled to the ground as the ghostly form of Lily-Anne continued to stand.

Kyle's body also fell to the ground as Pierre remained ethereal facing Lily-Anne.

Pierre rushed Lily-Anne but was halted before reaching her by the spirits of those she'd called just moments before, surrounding him. Ren and Chase pulled Aurora out of the way while Raven and Stone grabbed Kyle.

Brandon had appeared on the scene just as all of this was occurring. "What the hell is—"

Stone shushed him, handing the limp form of Kyle off to his big brother.

Aurora and Kyle were just coming out of their stupor, trying to make sense of what was happening before them.

"Now is your chance. Now is your time," Lily-Anne almost chanted to the others.

Pierre spun around, his features gaunt in fear.

"You've brought fear to each of us before ending our existence," the figure of Allison stated.

"I swore that you were innocent, but suffered along with you when you were found guilty of killing Lily-Anne. Now I stand with her and the others you have murdered so callously for your own amusement and pleasure." Jacob continued move forward with the others.

Lily-Anne stayed just outside of the circle as the others closed in. "You have hurt so many, and you have never cared. I had a life. We all had lives, and you took them from us for your own perverse pleasure. It's time for you to pay."

"Pay? How do you expect me to pay? I'm already dead, bitch." Pierre shrugged off his fear.

Jasper stepped up. "By your mistakes."

Pierre had to turn around to face Jasper. "What mistakes?"

"You're on sacred land, first off," Bianca calmly stated, though her eyes seemed to burn out of her ghostly figure.

"And we call upon our ancestors of this land to exact revenge," Shelby exclaimed, then started chanting. The others joined him as Lily-Anne entered the circle they made to surround him.

Pierre looked around as soon the ancestors of Lakota Sioux began to appear. Fearful of what they were going to do to his soul, Pierre lunged for Lily-Anne. "You were my first and my most enjoyable. You shall be my shield."

However, Lily-Anne pushed him back. "I'm no longer under your control. I'm no longer yours to do with any way you please, nor will I no longer be silent as you condemn others to my existence. Your time has come. Your time is now. No more, Pierre Hills, shall you destroy."

A white glow appeared from Lily-Anne's ethereal hands, the light spreading with the growing chanting, now increasing as those still alive joined in the chant.

The bright light seemed to burn Pierre, his ghostly spirit bursting into flames before dissipating into nothingness. Once Pierre was gone, one by one, the others also disappeared, though by going into the light.

Only Lily-Anne remained and she turned to

Aurora, who stood there in stunned silence.

"I'm sorry."

Aurora shook her head. Was a ghost actually speaking to her? "About what?"

"For using you. I entered your body in order to save Allison, but Pierre beat me there and I didn't have a strong enough hold. I only got into you better when you visited the Melodian. But even then, I couldn't stop him from killing Jasper, Shelby and Bianca. I tried, but I failed." Lily-Anne turned to face Chase. "Know I was not with her when you two fornicated. I gave you peace and privacy so everything that happened was only between the two of you." Lily-Anne looked up as a shaft of light hovered above her. She smiled, looking like an angel before she turned her attention back to Aurora.

"Have a happy life." Lily-Anne reached up and smiled. "My love. My husband. I'm coming home." And then she was gone.

Aurora's knees buckled and Chase reached out to catch her. Albeit, even he was a bit flabbergasted, as were those around them. `

It was Zonta who'd arrived with some of the other elders during the confrontation of the victims of Pierre who broke the silence. "We still have a few things to discuss. Please return to the sacred dance circle."

As she turned and headed away, Ren assisted Chase in bringing Aurora to them. Ren realized Chase had a few more bleeding cuts on him thanks to the battle he'd had with possessed Kyle. Brandon helped his brother and several followed them to the elders.

Chapter Nineteen

Within minutes, the group stood uneasily in front of the elders. None of them were sure what they were there for, nor what was about to occur next. They were all still trying to process what they'd seen and heard.

Zonta stood and walked past each of them slowly, pausing briefly until she reached Aurora.

"It'll be okay, child," she stated calmly in a soothing tone before her hand whipped up to place a piece of flowstone onto her forehead.

Aurora's eyes immediately rolled to the back of her head and her knees buckled. Chase caught her immediately, almost growling at Zonta for whatever she did to the woman he cared about and who had already been through so much.

Although he still held Aurora's limp form, Zonta spoke to her as if she were bright-eyed and alert.

"You are a vessel. Is anyone still here?"

A rich voice came through Aurora, who stood on her own. Although Chase was a bit hesitant, he let her go, remaining close in case she needed him again.

"I am. I know what you need."

"And what is that?" Zonta asked.

"A sacrifice. You can use me, Chayton Black Oak, or he who is more commonly known as Shelby."

"Thank you, Shelby. Your wisdom and your sacrifice is most generous."

"I didn't trust her. Because I hated her with my very being for who I thought killed my daughter. I can only make peace by taking the blame and setting her free."

"Just as she has set you and all the others free. You will be remembered," Zonta almost reverently replied.

Aurora's head nodded and then she collapsed again as Shelby released her body.

As she came to, she looked around questioningly. "Why am I always seeming to faint lately?"

"Your body is a vessel, and I'm sorry to say we

were using it to speak to our ancestors."

"Well, isn't that a nice how do you do? I don't go invading your body! How can you just have mine taken over?" She stood up angrily. "Look, either condemn me to death or whatever, otherwise, I'm out of here. I've had more than enough of *all* of you and these circus magical tricks I seem to be an unwitting accomplice for. Just give me back my camera and equipment and I'll be on my way."

Ren swiftly moved to grab all the evidence still in Apple's facilities and returned it to Aurora. "Everything is there but the switchblade. Evidence, you understand. Standing Bear and I will call the detectives in Deadwood to make sure you're cleared."

Zonta nodded, agreeing with Ren. "We've put you through enough to more than suffice the pictures you took. We know you will keep our secret, and you will make sure that the child will return to us when puberty hits, as only we can train and protect him. We ask nothing further of you."

Aurora nodded, grabbed her stuff and, without

any goodbyes, headed for her vehicle to drive back to Deadwood.

"Well, that was kinda rude." Brandon leaned over so only Chase would hear. "And you wanted to have her in your life? Fool." Moving over to Kyle, Brandon shoved his brother's shoulder and the two headed back to their tipi.

Chase followed them with his eyes, feeling Stone come up beside him. "She needs time to assimilate everything that just happened to her, and you need time to get your new wounds taken care of. I married a human female. Trust me. If you really care, doing anything and everything you can will make the difference."

"She doesn't seem to want to be with me, no matter how much time I give her."

"Meet her in Deadwood. In her world. Things might change, and if not, could you live knowing you didn't try everything you could?"

Chase sighed. "Thanks." He headed off to get his new cuts looked at, knowing the deepest cut of all couldn't be fixed by anyone except Aurora.

*   *   *   *

At the hotel, Aurora was met by Detectives Hansley and Collins. She rolled her eyes as she tiredly climbed the steps of the Franklin.

"Ms. Taylor?" Hansley stepped forward to block her way.

"Look. I'm exhausted and I'm hungry. Is this going to take long?"

"No, ma'am. I just wanted to let you know that Officer Standing Bear contacted us and told us what happened at the pow-wow. How they found the culprit, Shelby Black Oak. We wanted to apologize to you and let you know that you were free to go back home."

"Fine. Thanks." She headed up to her room. After dropping her bags, she ordered room service from the steakhouse downstairs and then went to freshen up.

She'd just finished changing her clothes when a knock on the door came. She was starving and grateful the food took less time than expected. However, it wasn't the meal she ordered but Chase at her door. She rolled her eyes.

"Come on. Seriously? Are you here to drag me back to your group? Did they change their minds about letting me go? Have I not been through enough?"

Chase sighed. "Not here to drag you back. Here to see if I could convince you one more time to marry me."

She spun around and headed back into the room, leaving the door opened. "Come on, Chase. We've been through all of this. The answer is no."

"Why? Do you think I'll make that awful of a husband? Am I that hideous to you because of what I am?"

She sat down, staring out the window overlooking Main Street. "I think you will make a wonderful husband. For someone."

"Just not you."

"Just not me."

"Why? I think I deserve an explanation."

Aurora hesitated. She wanted to say yes, but she didn't trust him or herself. "Guess 'it's me, not you,' won't be enough of an excuse?"

"No. It won't." He moved into the room, shutting the door behind him.

She wanted to give him several reasons but wasn't sure how to begin. One thing, though, she was never a liar. "A few years back I got engaged. Spent hundreds of dollars on the wedding of my dreams with the man of my dreams. And my dreams were left on the altar as he never showed. Then a few years later, I thought, this is the guy I'm supposed to be with. That's why Dennis never showed up. I'm supposed to be with Rick. But then on the night before our wedding, I caught Rick in bed with my maid-of-honor. I know I'm not a package for anyone, but I'll be damned if anyone is forced to marry me because I'm pregnant with their child."

"It's more than that," Chase started to say, but Aurora held up her hand, indicating for him to stop.

"You're right. There is more. There is you and your life. I heard they would make you give up the PBR. Something I know you thoroughly enjoy and already have to give up in a few years anyway. Why would I want to be the one responsible for taking what time you have away? And then there is your best friend, Brandon. He doesn't want me to be with you or even near the band. You said yourself that you have been besties for hundreds of years. I won't be responsible for coming between you two only to have you regret it down the road. Finally, Brandon and all of your band is here in South Dakota, and though this is a nice place to visit, I much prefer the city life of St. Louis." She moved around him and opened the door. "I don't think there is anything else to say, except I wish you all the best. Goodbye."

Chase hesitated, but she stared straight ahead, not even looking at him. He'd been rejected before, even by her, but this was the worst. "Know I'm only a phone call away if you ever need me."

He placed a card with his name and phone number on it as he passed by the table before he left the room, turning as she shut the door behind him.

She leaned heavily against the door, hating

what she did, but knowing it was the right choice. Aurora was unable to stop the flow of tears that suddenly streamed uncontrollably down her face as her heart broke. If her heart hurt this much, she knew it would only be worse should she have let him in more. She'd already had her heart broken twice before, but neither time was this poignant. She thought she'd loved Dennis and Rick, but she had been wrong. She was deeply, madly, no-going-back, head-over-heels in love with Chase, and the only thing she could do was to let him go so he could find the happiness that he deserved.

Chapter Twenty

The following morning, Chase stood out of the way and watched as Aurora drove away from the hotel. She hadn't seen him or known he was there. He didn't want to make things worse for her by letting her know he was watching. He wanted to be with her, keep her with him, but that's not what she wanted, and he wouldn't force anyone to stay with him if they didn't want to.

She'd turned down his proposal a multitude of times. He hoped she'd changed her mind once everything had been cleared up, but alas, she was determined to have her freedom and return to St. Louis without him.

His heart ached, and he balled his fists tightly at his side just to feel something other than the pain that coursed through his body. He thought he'd been in love before, but the feelings he had with Bianca paled in comparison to what he was going through now. Worse, she was carrying his child and he didn't know if Aurora would even acknowledge him as the father or not. Hell, for all he knew, she'd have an abortion while in St. Louis and move on with her life as if he never existed.

She'd promised him she would keep the child and that she wouldn't prevent his parental rights, but she knew nothing of what it meant to raise a shifter and the tribulations it would incur. When he'd mentioned it to her, she only nodded agreement and mumbled something about finding him and turning the child over to his care. But women were fickle and she had nine months to change her mind as she developed a motherly bond with the infant she carried in her womb.

"I won't marry you. Not now. Not ever." She repeated those words to him so often they were still ringing in his ears. What was he to do?

He told her the truth of what he was, what his people were, and she wanted nothing to do with him or his kind. At least she agreed to keep their secret quiet. "Who'd believe me anyways? I'd be locked up in some hospital for the insane if I told anyone about any of you. Truth be told, I'm still not sure anything I saw was actually real. Changing forms, ghosts, possession. It's all mind boggling and surreal."

How was he supposed to respond to that? To outsiders it had to be strange and incomprehensible. So he stood by and let her go, despite everything his heart and soul were telling him.

Even though the vehicle was no longer in sight, he continued to stare at the direction in which she left. Finally, he turned slowly, checked to make sure no one was watching, shifted into a hawk and flew back to the encampment. They had one day left of the pow-wow before everyone would head home and he, among the others of his band, would clean the area. Many of the ceremonies had been disrupted, but they were not too far behind from the overall competition and celebratory dances.

For the first time in a couple of hundred years, Chase had no interest in the festivities. Actually, he had no interest in anything. When he'd left her after the PBR, sure to never see her again, it'd been hard. But he had an obligation to his band to make sure the pow-wow went off wonderfully. Then she had to show up. And he learned she was carrying his child. And she learned about what he and his people were. And everything changed. For a few moments, he had seen a future with her. A family. A home. Things he'd not allowed himself to think of since Bianca tore his heart out all those centuries ago. Now Bianca was dead and the woman he loved was gone, not wanting him to be a part of her life.

The day passed with the contests, the dances, the prayers, yet Chase wasn't mentally there. He watched, prepared, cleaned, and moved out of obligation, nothing more. He finally retired when he was too exhausted to do more than stand on his feet.

Still, Chase couldn't sleep. His mind raced of thoughts of Aurora. Frustrated, he headed out of his tipi to watch the sun rise.

He heard steps behind him, but paid no never mind until Brandon and Kyle sat on either side of him.

"I'm sorry." Kyle crossed his legs as he sat down.

"Me too," Brandon added.

"I know. It's not your fault. Not entirely. I don't blame either of you."

"I'm just glad it…he is gone. You can't imagine how it is to hate yourself and all those around you just 'cause we're Natives. To hate women. ME? Man. I love women. And here this thing gets inside of me and wants to kill 'em."

Chase gave a twitch of a smile at the latter part of Kyle's words. "Yeah. You're a bit too much of a man-whore to women."

"We're headed to the Cave of the Winds later. For a pure cleansing. To make sure every little iota of Pierre's essence is eliminated. Back to where everything began with White Calf Woman. Will you come with us, bro?" Brandon didn't look up, finding the blades of grass more interesting than his companions. "I know I owe you a huge apology. About Aurora. There was something about her I didn't like. Something I didn't trust. I hadn't realized she was possessed, too, and I was reacting to that. I listened to Kyle, not knowing he was possessed. I believed my brother when he spewed so many lies about Aurora, fueling my hatred and distrust. I didn't want you hurt so I tried to keep you from her. Instead, I hurt you worse because of the deceit of a dead man. I can't apologize to you enough."

Chase slapped him on the arm. "I get it. She's human. She was a danger and a threat, as is. I didn't know about the other stuff. It's probably why she found me interesting at all to begin with. Like you, the possession probably screwed up her mind, and now she has to bear the consequences of it by carrying my child. And yeah, I'll come with you two to Cave of the Winds for a purification cleansing." He knew some of what he said were exaggerations as Lily-Anne, Zonta, and even Aurora told him otherwise, but he didn't know what was really true anymore other than Aurora didn't want him, was gone, and he watched her go.

"Great. Thanks." Brandon returned the punch to Chase's arm.

They sat quietly for a little longer before Kyle stood up. "I'm going to get ready. I'll see you both in a bit."

Brandon watched him go then stood as well. "Look. I ain't pleased about all my behavior towards Aurora, but she's carrying your kid and I can tell you really care for her. After we finish the cleansing, I think you should go to St. Louis to be with her."

"I can't leave the band."

"Why not? In a way you already have with the ranch on the border. And as for the PBR, you can still ride and compete, just make weekends out of it. She ain't willing to leave her home and move here, then you need to move there."

"She doesn't want me. She turned down my proposal several times."

"Because you were asking her to give up everything. You go to her, and you are giving up reservation life to be with her. Personally, I don't think it's that bad of a deal. And you still have the ranch you can come home to for visits or whatever."

Chase thought about those wise words. He never did say he would go with her. Give up his life for her. Live in her world. He just expected her to do that for him. But this was a new day and age and women had more rights and freedom than they did of old. Why couldn't he go to her? Why couldn't he ask again, but this time showing her he would do anything to be with her, not the other way around? Would it make a difference? Or did she really detest him and want nothing to do with him? Was her...infatuation just that? Or part of her possession? Or something more?

"I'll help you pack when we finish. You'd be a fool if you didn't give it your all on her terms not your own. She really cares for you, Chase. She wasn't possessed during the time she spent with you. Lily-Anne said she left you two alone so you could be together. So why wouldn't she want to be with you now?" Brandon made the decision he was going while Chase was still thinking about it, then departed before Chase could argue.

Chase sat and continued to watch the sunrise, wondering if the future with Aurora would be as bright as the orb's illumination, or if once again he'd be crushed by her refusal.

Chapter Twenty-One

Aurora opened her studio last night, spending the time developing the pictures she needed to work on today. She had a lab set up next door to her gallery, so it was convenient to print out what she wanted and move them next door. The last thing she desired was to be alone in her apartment with thoughts of what she gave up. She'd been back in her home city for a week and she was missing Chase as much now as she did when she left him. What choice did she have? He would've either changed his mind about being with her at the last minute when she'd finally trusted him, or he'd be giving up everything to be with her and then later regret it *and* her.

Her hand went to her belly. A life was supposed to be there. A life that was unique and different from hers. How was she supposed to cope on her own with things she still couldn't believe existed in the world? She moved around her studio. She had printed all of her pictures, and although she was still going over the majority of them, she had her favorites picked out and framed. Today she wanted to hang them, moving some of the other ones that hadn't sold to a different position in her studio, hoping they would gain interest with a different location.

With care, she hung her new pieces, but they only made her melancholy, wishing she hadn't left South Dakota or Chase. But she couldn't stay, and she couldn't marry the only man who meant anything to her. She couldn't stand another broken heart, nor could she risk being despised.

Hearing the clang of the bell over the door, she grabbed a rag to wipe her hands and greet her prospective customer. Maybe moving those older photos up front garnered some interest after all. However, when she looked up, she was astounded at the person who stood in her studio.

Chase pulled his hat off, gripping the rim in his hands nervously. He looked almost sheepish as he looked around before locking his eyes on hers. He wasn't sure what kind of a reception he was going to get and she was too surprised to do more than gape at him.

After a few moments of awkward silence, Chase cleared his throat. "Aurora. You're looking well."

She blinked a few more times before she finally found enough of her voice to reply. "Thanks? Um…what? What are you doing here?"

"Look, I know you don't want me, but I…I can't just let you go."

Dawning came over her face. "Oh. The baby. I wasn't going to cut him or her out of your life entirely. You have every right to get to know your child when they are born. You didn't have to come here to make sure of it. I'm not that kind of person."

He ran his hand through his hair while his other clutched the rim of his hat tighter. "I didn't think you were going to prevent me from seeing our child once they were born."

"Then why are you here? To check up on me? To make sure I don't tell anyone about you and your people?"

He sighed. "No. The elders believe that you

will maintain our secret. Raven and Hope convinced them to believe your integrity. You have nothing to fear from any of us."

"And you all have nothing to fear from me."

He gave his head a single nod, then looked around the room, moving to examine the various photos she had in her studio.

Her eyes watched him closely, unsure of everything. Unsure if this was even real and he was really in her studio. "How? I mean, how did you find me?"

Chase stopped and turned back at her, pulling his eyes away from a photo that he really liked of a foggy morning along a deserted road while a beam of light pierced the haze that swirled around the ground. It had an ethereal quality to it and he admired this particular picture. Albeit, everything he'd seen thus far he really liked.

"When we had your camera bag at the campsite, you had some business cards in one of the pockets. I'm afraid I stole one."

"Ah." She didn't know what else to say. He

still hadn't answered why he was in St. Louis, much less in her studio.

He rounded a corner and stopped, his intake of air his only expression of incredulity at what he beheld. It was obviously the space she used as her office, but the pictures surrounding her desk were nothing of what he'd anticipated. He turned to look at her, her cheeks bright red in embarrassment, her eyes averted.

He turned about to the half dozen enlarged photos, examining them more closely. "I didn't even know you took these."

All of them were of him, either profiled or looking down, his hat covering a portion of his face. One was when he was riding Devil, his body arched back, his one arm in the air, the other clasping the rope about the bull. The picture was beautiful and could've been used for an advertisement to the PBR. She had one of him in black and white, the shadows and light playing against his form that enhanced his muscles, the hat tipped way down so only his chin showed. She had that one front and center, so large it was almost lifelike. "Are they for your personal use or to sell?"

She shuffled her feet slightly, hanging her head before she responded softly. "My use only."

He turned back to her. In two steps he was in front of her, using his forefinger to lift her chin so her eyes met his. "I thought you hated me. That you couldn't stand the sight of me."

"I don't hate you. I've never hated you. Or what you are."

"Then why push me away? Why did you turn my proposals down? I thought it was because you couldn't stand what I am. What our child will be."

"No. No." She shook her head empathically. "I can't marry you because I didn't want you to give up your world and I couldn't live in yours."

"My world? You mean shifting?"

"That. And the PBR. And the land you've only known. Whether or not you are gifted as the rest of your band and the others at the pow-wow, you're still Native American, and the things you told me, the things I learned about your race, your culture, over the previous few days we had together made me realize I couldn't ask you to leave any of it. But my life is here. My studio, my friends. I...I'm not quite willing to give them up. At least not yet."

"I don't need the PBR. In fact, I only had a little longer I could compete anyways before I would have to leave in order to not let my secret longevity be discovered. I can leave the reservation and my ranch without a problem. What I can't seem to live without is you."

"You're just saying that because I'm carrying your child."

Exasperated, he sighed, a slight growl rumbling deep within his chest, making the sigh sound more like a snort. "I couldn't fucking care less you're carrying my child right now. Don't get me wrong. I'm actually thrilled at the thought of being a father, but *you* are what I want in my life. Do you think all the time I spent with you was for a baby? I didn't want to sleep with you because you might or might not get pregnant. Honestly, that wasn't even a viable thought. What I wanted was to be with you in the most intimate way possible. A memory I hoped would last me a couple of hundred years. I've never felt for someone as I do you. Your spirit, your fire, your passion, those are what drives me. Those are what calls me to continue to be by your side. I burn for you in need and desire. I want you. Every part of you, and I'm willing to give up my life in order to be with you just a few minutes more. My heart ached when I left you. I hurt so much I couldn't even face you because I knew, right then and there, that if you were awake, I wouldn't go."

Chase fell on his knees and wrapped his arms around her waist, laying his head against her belly. "I'm not one to beg. I've never done anything or fought for anything as important as this. But I... I'm in love with you and I will beg every hour of every day if that's what it takes for you to accept me." He lifted his head up to peer into her eyes. "I came here for you. I want nothing more than to have you in my life. But know that I'm not leaving you or St. Louis. Wherever you are, I will be close by and I'll always respect your decision."

"And what of your PBR and other stuff?"

"The PBR goes all over the country. I can fly in and out as need be or retire all together. I still own my ranch, so I won't be abandoning my band or my history, and should you ever wish it, we have a place to go, whether for a visit or vacation or whatever." He reached into his back pocket and pulled out a velvet box. "Please, please marry me. Let me be a part of your life. Now and forever."

"Forever? I'm human. I'm not going to have the lifespan you have. How can I say yes?"

"You can. It's part of our marriage ritual. I can give you some of my life force and it will extend yours. Literally tie yours to mine." He opened the box, showing off the antique-looking diamond ring.

She had never been one for the classic engagement ring, but this was unusual and breathtaking.

"Please, Aurora. Don't say no this time. Marry me. Make me the happiest man alive."

Tears welled up in her eyes, the ring and Chase becoming bleary. All the reasons she'd had to turn him down he now brushed away, and there was no reason left not to give in to what she also wanted more than anything. Her throat tightened. Knowing she couldn't speak in her current state, she nodded. He smiled and jumped up, lifting her off her feet, crushing her to his chest, his lips slamming against hers, forcing his tongue into her mouth. "Mine," he growled.

And that's when she knew her premonitions of seeing Chase in a field, laughing, surrounded by children, were her children…their children, and everything she'd seen was going to come true. Finally finding her voice, she nodded again. "Yours. Always."

Epilogue

Five years later

The sun was high but hidden. The light streaming in beams from between the clouds gave the area an almost ethereal appearance. A soft breeze blew over the grasslands, rustling the few blades of green mixed with dandelions and some scattered wildflowers strewn about. The weather was spring-like and warm.

It was quiet overall. A few chirping birds, an occasional cricket or two. It was too early for the nuisance bugs to be flying about as the world was still waking up from the cold of winter.

Aurora pulled the cardigan closer around her as she walked alone, enjoying the peacefulness of the late morning. There weren't many times in her life of late that she had several moments to herself, so she took advantage when she could. She found herself amazed that it was these peaceful times she felt to be the loneliest.

Then she heard the squeals and screams. She ran around the mound of dirt blocking her view from the commotion going on, stopping short. She stood silently to watch, bringing her camera up as she snapped a couple of pictures. When she pulled the camera down, she smiled.

In front of her was her vision come true. Chase sitting on the ground as he held their newest born against his broad chest. Chase would occasionally lift Brandon Junior in the air and fly him like a bird, making BJ giggle as he flailed about before returning to the safety of his father's arms. Meanwhile, the eldest, Colt, chased his little sister, Lily around their father, squealing and screaming in mock horror as they did so.

Aurora couldn't have felt more blessed. Everything she wanted, everything she dreamed of was right in front of her, and for her, it was perfect. She had married Chase the traditional Native American way, and in return, he gave her a bit of his life force so her life span was now tied to his and she would live beyond her years as a human. The idea of being around for hundreds of years still boggled her mind, but Chase was there to help her through any and all of her anxieties. Best of all, Chase was there, by her side. Loving her. And she couldn't have wanted anything more than that.

She was so engrossed in watching her family she hadn't realized two others approached her from behind.

Brandon and Kyle came up behind Aurora, startling her when Brandon grabbed her in a bear hug, lifting her off her feet and flinging her over his shoulder as she squealed. She knew she wasn't in any danger with Chase so close, but still she was shocked by no longer having her feet on the ground. Once he set her down, Kyle stepped up, giving her a traditional hug. Stepping back from the two men she'd grown to love as much as Chase did, she led the two men over to Chase, grabbing Brandon's arm in the process. "It's about time you met your namesake. And Kyle," she slipped her free arm around his waist, "you've yet to meet your godson."

Chase stood and handed BJ over to Brandon, his smile as big as the outdoors. He gave Kyle a man hug with a slap on the back before he pulled back. "Glad you two could make it. Colt and Lily have been wanting me to fire up the grill for the last thirty minutes, saying how hungry they were."

Kyle knelt down as he called the other two children over with the promise of lollipops shaped in feathers. Squealing, they gave their Uncle Kyle a hug and dashed over with promises they would wait a little longer.

"What? I don't even get a hello?" Brandon growled teasingly.

The two children put their candy and their heads down as they approached Brandon to give him a hug and kiss on the cheek in hopes that would supplicate Uncle Brandon that they could continue to enjoy their treat. At first, Brandon refused to let them off the hook so easily, but after a moment, and with BJ tugging his hair, Brandon smiled and told them to go off and play.

Aurora stepped back to let the men talk and get acquainted with the children. They had just arrived in South Dakota, back at the property they owned, to settle down for the next couple of months. There were a few Native rituals that BJ had to be inducted into, and several lessons the children would learn while they visited the reservation lands, life lessons passed from the elders to the next generation.

Chase and Aurora had settled down into a good routine. They stayed in St. Louis during the winter and came to Chase's ranch in the summer for a couple of months. Chase had just finished his last season in the PBR events, retiring before humans began to notice any lack of changes.

Instead, he turned to marketing after going to an online college to get a degree in business management and marketing. Now he was even more effective in helping Aurora with pushing her photography and her studio.

As Aurora stepped back, her vision swam slightly. Again she was at an open gravesite, but this time, there were two people standing beside it. She recognized Lily-Anne, and the male gazing lovingly into her eyes must be the preacher husband she had loved and lost all those years ago. Lily-Anne turned to Aurora and smiled. "Thank you.

Because of you, I was able to finally stop Pierre and he is in the hell he deserves. But I also thank you for remembering me in naming your daughter, Lily. I know you did it because of me."

"Although I didn't know it, you were a part of me. Because of you, I stayed behind to watch the pow-wow, which brought Chase back to me. I'm glad I was able to give you peace."

Kyle turned and looked questioningly at Chase. "Dude. What's up with your woman? She's talking to herself."

Chase laughed. "Did you know, my beautiful wife had a gift before we even met. It's why Lily-Anne was able to possess her so easily. Aurora has visions. Not often, but they do come. Kind of like a premonition. Though, from her words, I've a feeling this one might be a vision from the past. Either way, she's even more special than we'd given her credit for originally. Turns out, one of her ancient ancestors was Osage Indian. Not enough for her to claim any legal bonds, but enough for her to retain some of her Native heritage. I'm trying to work with her in strengthening her powers, but it's a huge work in progress. This is one of the few times I've seen her vision in action in the last few months. But with the pregnancy and all, we just haven't had much time to practice."

"With three kids, and I know you're working on making more, I doubt you have much time for any practice. For her visions, I mean." Brandon chuckled as he bounced BJ on his hip.

Kyle rolled his eyes. "You can be so gross, big brother. And you've had BJ long enough. Let me see my godson." He reached for BJ just as Colt and Lily tackled each of Brandon's legs alternatively to drag Brandon to a game of tag.

Chase took a few steps away from the group, letting the kids visit with their uncles while he moved closer to Aurora, but not enough to break whatever she was seeing.

"What's the grave about? This isn't my present, is it?" Aurora asked Lily-Anne.

Lily-Anne smiled at her. "No. It's my husband's grave. It was the last time I saw him, and my heart was buried with him. When I was with you, my memory crossed over into your vision. I apologize for that. For all I used your body for. I am sorry."

"You did what you had to do, Lily-Anne. Had you asked, I would've agreed to let you use it. Your mission was important. I'm just sorry we couldn't stop him sooner. But why have you returned after all this time? Do you need my body again?"

Lily-Anne shook her head. "No. Time is not the same here as it is for the living. It is more fluid. To you, it is years. To us, just minutes, days. I will leave now. We will leave. I just wanted you to know the truth. You are why we succeeded."

Before Aurora could say another word, Lily-Anne, her husband and the gravesite disappeared as rapidly as they appeared. She turned around to find Chase behind her.

"Are you okay, my love?" Concerned edged his voice.

"Yes. A visit more than a vision. I'll tell you all about it later. For now, I believe we have some grilling to do and some family to spend time with."

"Maybe. But they can wait a moment. I need to do something first."

She cocked her head quizzically, her eyebrows furrowed. "What?"

He pulled her close and wrapped his hand behind her head. "Kiss you," he murmured before he pressed his lips hard against hers, his hands cupping her ass.

He growled. "Mine."

She licked his lips and nipped his nose. "Forever and always, my love. Forever and always."

ABOUT THE AUTHOR

Ms. Hawks has always been interested in writing in some form or other, including writing for a local newspaper. Deciding to become more knowledgeable, she headed back to school and received her Master's Degree in Ancient Civilizations, Native American History and United States History.

It was at this time she got involved in role playing on FaceBook, which gave her ample opportunities to grow and hone her writing ability.

She lives in the suburbs of Chicago with her four companions, all males... cats. She travels as much as she can to various Author/Reader conventions and loves to meet established fans and make new ones, some of which she considers friends more than fans. Check out her social media sites to follow her.

WebSite: AuthorLauraHawks.com
Twitter: AuthorLHawks
FB Author page:
https://www.facebook.com/LauraHawks-
249262585192270/?fref=ts
FB Fan Group: Hawks Flock:
https://www.facebook.com/groups

For Further Information:

Dead Files. Season 3: Episode 10. 2013.

Ghost Adventures. Season 10: Episode 11. 2015.

PBS: American Experience. Native Americans and Mount Rushmore. 2016.

McAllister, Frances A. *The Lakota Sioux: Their Ceremonies and Recreations*. 1968.

Shadley, Mark, and Josh Wennes. *Haunted Deadwood: a True Wild West Ghost Town*. Haunted America, 2012.

Bryant, Jerry L. and Fifer, Barbara. *Deadwood's Al Swearington: Manifest Evil in the Gem Theater*. 2018.

Gibbon, Guy. *The Sioux? The Dakota and Lakota Nations*. 2002

Pevar, Stephen L. *The Rights of Indians and Tribes*.2012.

Greene, Jerome A. *Lakota and Cheyenne: Indian Vies of the Great Sioux War, 1876-1877*. 2000

DeWall, Robb. *Carving A Dream: Crazy Horse Memorial Now in Progress in the Black Hills of South Dakota*. 1995.